ALBERT R. BROCCOLI's EON PRODUCTIONS presents
PIERCE BROSNAN
as IAN FLEMING'S JAMES BOND 007 in

TOMORROW NEVER DIES

ALBERT R. BROCCOLI's EON PRODUCTIONS

presents PIERCE BROSNAN

as IAN FLEMING'S JAMES BOND 007 in

"TOMORROW NEVER DIES"

JONATHAN PRYCE   MICHELLE YEOH   TERI HATCHER

JOE DON BAKER and JUDI DENCH

Costume Designer	LINDY HEMMING
Music by	DAVID ARNOLD
Director of Photography	ROBERT ELSWIT
Production Designer	ALLAN CAMERON
Line Producer	ANTHONY WAYE
Written by	BRUCE FEIRSTEIN
Produced by	MICHAEL G. WILSON and BARBARA BROCCOLI
Directed by	ROGER SPOTTISWOODE
Title Song Performed by	SHERYL CROW

DISTRIBUTED BY MGM DISTRIBUTION CO. AND

UNITED INTERNATIONAL PICTURES

Tomorrow Never Dies

A novel by Raymond Benson
Based upon the screenplay by Bruce Feirstein

BOULEVARD BOOKS, NEW YORK

TOMORROW NEVER DIES

A Boulevard Book / published by arrangement with
Glidrose Publications Limited

Tomorrow Never Dies © 1997 Danjaq. LLC and
United Artists Corporation ALL RIGHTS RESERVED.

007 Gun Symbol Logo © 1962 Danjaq. LLC and
United Artists Corporation ALL RIGHTS RESERVED.

Photograph of Pierce Brosnan © 1997 Danjaq. LLC and
United Artists Corporation ALL RIGHTS RESERVED.

Back Cover Illustration © 1997 Danjaq. LLC and
United Artists Corporation ALL RIGHTS RESERVED.

PRINTING HISTORY
Boulevard edition / December 1997

The Putnam Berkley World Wide Web site address is
http://www.berkley.com

ISBN: 1-57297-345-5

BOULEVARD
Boulevard Books are published by The Berkley Publishing Group,
a member of Penguin Putnam Inc.,
200 Madison Avenue, New York, New York 10016.
BOULEVARD and its logo are trademarks
belonging to Berkley Publishing Corporation.

PRINTED IN THE UNITED STATES OF AMERICA

10 9 8 7 6 5 4 3 2 1

For my fellow board members at the
Ian Fleming Foundation:
John Cork, Lucy Fleming, Kate Fleming Grimond,
Peter Janson-Smith, Doug Redenius, David A. Reinhardt,
Mike Van Blaricum, and Dave Worrall

IN MEMORY OF
NICHOLAS FLEMING

Special thanks to:
Barbara Broccoli, Michael G. Wilson,
John Parkison, and Meg Simmonds of EON Productions;
Elizabeth Beier; Carolyn Caughey; Dan Harvey;
James McMahon; David A. Reinhardt; Corinne B. Turner;
and Mike Vincitore

Tomorrow Never Dies

ONE

The Flea Market From Hell

The snow had covered the area and made traveling treacherous, but it didn't keep important business from taking place. They had come from different parts of Europe and the Middle East to make their deals, trade, haggle, and—they hoped—return home with bargains.

The isolated landing strip in the Khyber Pass, just at the border of Afghanistan and Pakistan, was the perfect marketplace. It was a narrow, winding passage through the Safed Koh mountains of the Hindu Kush range, enabling travelers to cross the daunting terrain between the two countries. The Khyber Pass is a location rich in history. In the fifth century B.C., Darius I of Persia marched through it to the Indus River. Rudyard Kipling captured the British era of the region in his poetry. At an altitude of 3,500 feet, the gap in the mountains was forged by two small rivers that cut between the cliffs of shale and limestone. A caravan track and hard-surface road were put in place years ago, and a railroad on the

Pakistan side goes through thirty-four tunnels and ninety-four bridges and culverts.

A plateau in the Pass surrounded by the mountains served quite adequately as a landing strip, and the terrorist factions met there every other month to buy and sell. It was the only time that a truce was called, vendettas were canceled, and suspicions were laid aside. It was a convention for mercenaries, killers, religious fanatics, reactionaries, and profiteers: a flea market of terror. Everything could be had if the price was right: Scud missiles, Hungarian mortars, AK-47s, grenades, chemical weapons, helicopters, and even two MiG-29 Fulcrums—fully fuelled, armed and ready to go. The only things missing were a floor-plan handout for every guest, company names and logos identifying who was selling what, beautiful spokeswomen displaying the merchandise, and shuttle bus transportation from the parking lot.

No one was counting, but at least a hundred men showed up for the event. Invitations went through third parties and some of the visitors traveled circuitous routes to attend. The affair was organized by a mysterious entrepreneurial group that received payment from all those attending. There were rumors that the organizers were from Germany, but that wasn't certain and no one really cared. As long as adequate protection was provided, the guests were happy to be there. Once they saw the armed guards and the radar dish mounted with infrared Gatling guns, the conventioneers could haggle furiously without interruption. It was the best security money could buy.

Little did the terrorists know, however, that security had been breached. The entire flea market was being watched by elite members of the British military and intelligence staff in London. Someone present at the site had a concealed video camera and was sending a direct signal by satellite.

M, the head of MI6; Bill Tanner, her chief of staff; Russian General Bukharin; the British Admiral Roebuck; and a handful of other military brass sat in fascination in front of monitors in the Ministry of Defence situation room. General Bukharin had been invited into the British intelligence headquarters against Admiral Roebuck's wishes, but M insisted that he should see what was happening. Roebuck was one of the several military powerhouses who never quite got used to the head of MI6 being a woman.

The situation room was large and cavernous. It was hexagonal, and cinema-sized video screens on the walls surrounded the men and women who worked there. In the middle of the floor were banks of computers, desks, telephones, and various other communications links to the outside world. This was where Britain's first line of defence began. The big decisions were made in the situation room, and if something really serious came up, then the minister of defence would attend as well.

The terrorist flea market in Afghanistan was not particularly serious, but it warranted enough concern that the Russian general be allowed inside the sacred walls to watch. Once news from MI6's man in the field reached them that the weapons exchange would indeed take place, Admiral Roebuck ordered HMS *Chester* to patrol the Gulf of Oman. He was quite prepared to order the ship to fire a cruise missile at the site, effectively ending the bimonthly exchange of the devil's playtoys.

Bill Tanner was a longtime veteran of the Secret

Service, the chief of staff when the former M, Sir Miles Messervy, was in charge. Sir Miles had retired two years ago and had been succeeded by the formidable new M. Small in stature but sharp and alert, Tanner wore a headset that provided direct communication to the camera operator at the secret site, and used a red laser pen to point out to the spellbound audience items of interest on the larger-than-life image.

"As we suspected, a regular terrorist swap meet," he confirmed. "A Chinese Long March Scud, a French A-17 attack helicopter, a pair of Russian mortars—"

"Stolen!" interrupted General Bukharin, obviously incensed.

"—and the crates look like American rifles, Chilean mines, and German explosives," Tanner continued. He looked at M and raised his eyebrows. "Fun for the whole family."

M squinted her eyes. "I.D.s?"

Tanner spoke into his headset. "Black Rook to White Knight. Zoom in on those people on the right, would you please?"

The group watched as the video image panned to a view of one of the arms traders. Tanner pressed a button that prompted the computer to zoom in and begin a facial matching program. Thousands of images blurred past in a split second, then stopped on a man's mug shot. A dossier appeared alongside.

Tanner quickly summarized the information. "Gustav Meinholtz. Former East German STASI agent. He's now working freelance out of Teheran." The man had a long face, dark hair, glasses, and hollow cheeks.

The camera moved and zeroed in on another face. The facial matching program went through its tricks again.

4

"Satoshi Isagura. Chemical expert. He's wanted for the Tokyo subway attack. Currently working for the insurgent force in Zaire." Isagura was Japanese, thin, with closely cropped hair and a receding hairline. He sported a Fu Manchu mustache and was quite sinister-looking indeed.

Next, the camera focused on four men negotiating over a makeshift desk of crates. Three of the men were Eastern European, but the fourth—a sour, heavy, bearded man in his late forties or early fifties—might have been Indian or Pakistani. He wore a long, heavy coat and scarf, and a Russian-style fur cap over his ears. If a bulldog could grow whiskers, it might have resembled the man pictured on the huge wall monitor. He signaled impatiently for his bodyguards to open a briefcase full of cash. Tanner punched up the facial mapping program and the man's dossier appeared.

"Henry Gupta. Well well. He practically invented techno-terrorism. He's been on the FBI's most-wanted list since he nearly wiped out the whole of Berkeley, California, in 1967. He used to be a radical, then became an anarchist. Now he works for cash."

On the screen, Gupta was given a small oblong red box in return for the money. He opened it, but the lid obscured the box's contents from the viewers in London.

"Zoom in on that, can you?" M snapped.

Tanner worked the zoom. Luckily, Gupta turned to speak to someone, and the device in the box was revealed.

"Well, gentlemen," M declared, "we will be dining out on that for many years. I can't wait to show this to the CIA."

Admiral Roebuck shrugged. He didn't care much for

spy stuff. Lacking any semblance of a sense of humour, Roebuck was the epitome of Royal Navy stiffness. He was the type of man who liked to be in control, and he never let anyone forget it. Roebuck was in his fifties, tall, broad-shouldered, and wore a perpetual frown on his face that prompted M to comment behind his back that the admiral always looked as if he were chronically constipated.

Admiral Roebuck turned to his fellow officers and asked, "You saw that radar-controlled Gatling gun, General?"

Bukharin nodded. "Yes. Also the short-range mortars." The Russian's English was remarkably good. General Bukharin was a handsome man pushing sixty, and he had tremendous energy that made him seem much younger. He was intelligent, too, and his comments and observations always seemed to be the most sensible. M had commented to Tanner the evening before that of all the men in the situation room, she respected Bukharin the most, despite the fact that she perceived that he shared the other men's attitude toward her. It was clear that he thought the situation room was no place for a woman, even if it was a British situation room.

"There is enough there to start a world war, or at the very least, a revolution somewhere," Bukharin added.

"All the more reason to go with Plan B, don't you think?" Roebuck asked rhetorically. He said to Tanner, "Tell your man to drop back."

"You are right," Bukharin said. "And my troops are still fogbound in any event. By the time it clears, this—what is it, 'swap meet'?—could be over."

"Very well, then," Roebuck concurred. He had already made up his mind anyway. It was time for him to exert his authority. He reached for the red phone, but M felt compelled to say something.

"Admiral, I recognize that this is a military matter—"

"Yes, it is, M, and believe me—" Roebuck stopped and spoke into the phone, "HMS *Chester*—"

"Black Rook to White Knight," Tanner spoke into the headset. "Black King is going for the naval option."

"—we are concerned as you are about the surrounding villages," Roebuck resumed saying to M, "but they're at least two miles away. The accuracy of the cruise missile is within two *yards*."

Amused, General Bukharin asked, "Are you concerned for the health of these terrorists, madam?"

M glared at him. "I am concerned that we fully understand the situation. That's why we put our man in there."

Roebuck barked into the phone, "Black King to White Bishop. Authorization to fire."

Approximately 2,500 miles away, HMS *Chester* received Admiral Roebuck's orders. The *Chester* was a type 23 Duke class frigate that was equipped with eight McDonnell Douglas Harpoon 2-quad launchers for surface-to-surface missiles, and a British Aerospace Seawolf GWS 26 Mod 1 VLS for surface-to-air missiles. She had been on patrol in the Arabian Sea when the call had been put through hours earlier for her to move north to the Gulf of Oman. She was now on full alert.

On the bridge, the captain picked up the intercom and sent a clear message to the operations room. "Weapons authorized. Prepare to fire. On my count: Five. Four. Three. Two—"

The launcher on deck rotated into position and the cruise missile blasted off with precision.

"Missile away!" the firing officer in the ops room shouted into the intercom.

Back in the Ministry of Defence situation room, the observers could now see a different video screen displaying a satellite view of the missile's path and progress. They could also hear everything transmitted on the *Chester*'s intercom. General Bukharin was impressed. He would have to speak to the President about upgrading their own situation room.

"Time to target: four minutes, eight seconds," the firing officer reported. The distance from the frigate to the secret base in the Khyber Pass was roughly eight hundred miles.

Bill Tanner spoke urgently into his headset. "White Knight! Four minutes to impact! Get out of there!"

Something came through on the headset and Tanner frowned. He stepped closer to the monitor displaying the terrorist flea market. Blocking the view of a MiG was a jeep in the foreground.

"Yes, damn it, I know what it is!" Tanner said into the headset. "It's a *jeep*! Now get out of— No! You're not going to wait, you can't wait!"

M, sensing the urgency in Tanner's voice, stepped forward and focused on the monitor with the jeep. The others were too busy watching the track of the missile on the other monitor to pay any attention to the drama unfolding a couple of feet away.

The *Chester*'s firing officer reported, "Time to target: four minutes."

Admiral Roebuck turned to M with a smile. "All's well that ends well, don't—"

"Shut up," M said sternly.

The admiral was too astonished to be angry. He turned involuntarily to look at the monitor M was staring at.

The jeep on the monitor pulled away, revealing the MiG's wing. Now they all could see what their agent in the field could see and why he wasn't moving from the spot.

"Good God!" The admiral swallowed. "Is that—"

Tanner answered him, "A Soviet SB-5 nuclear torpedo!" The instrument was fixed to the MiG's wing.

M barked, "Order them to abort the missile."

General Bukharin's horrified expression confirmed Tanner's identification. "*Zabag garoshki!*"

Tanner spoke into the headset, "Right, White Knight. We see it, good work. Now get the hell out! Move!"

Admiral Roebuck grabbed the red phone again. "HMS *Chester,* urgent!" He turned to the general and asked, "The missile can't set it off, can it?"

Bukharin shrugged. "It might! And even if it doesn't, there's enough plutonium to make Chernobyl look like a picnic. Radiation! All over the mountains! In the snowpack, the water supply—"

"The village!" Tanner reminded them. "Can it be evacuated?"

"In three minutes?" Bukharin said with wide eyes. "In the middle of the mountains?"

Roebuck shouted into the phone, "Black King to White Bishop—abort missile! Abort missile!"

On the bridge of the *Chester,* the captain repeated the admiral's instructions on the intercom. "Abort missile!"

The firing officer pressed the Abort button but nothing happened. "Sir, I pressed the destruct but the missile is in the mountains now."

Suddenly, the Ministry of Defence situation room

9

burst into a frenzied beehive of activity. People were rushing about, shouting and grabbing phones.

"Try it again!" the admiral shouted into the red phone. "Keep trying!"

Tanner spoke to his agent in the field, "White Knight? Why are you still transmitting?"

M sat looking at the monitor amid the disciplined, military version of utter panic. She remained calm— unnaturally so. For she and Tanner knew something that the others didn't.

She whispered to her chief of staff, "That camera is no longer manned."

Tanner replied, "Good, then. At least *he*'s out of it."

"You should know by now—he's *never* where you think he is."

The two terrorist guards sat around the fire keeping warm, completely unaware that they were minutes from certain death. They had met for the first time at the weapons exchange, having been recruited from diverse areas of Europe. It was important that no one who worked for the organizers could be traced. If it hadn't been for all the weapons of destruction scattered around them in the background, they might have seemed like tramps at a makeshift fire.

One of the guards casually looked around at the silent mountain range behind him and put a cigarette to his mouth. A gold Dunhill lighter appeared in front of his face and obligingly lit the end of the cigarette. The guard inhaled once and glanced over to see which friendly associate had done him a favour. Before he could identify the man, a fist knocked him flat.

In one fluid movement, James Bond picked up the

fallen guard's gun and smashed the second guard's face.

"Filthy habit," Bond said to the unconscious first guard.

There wasn't much time. If he was going to get out of there alive, he didn't have time to stop and analyze different strategies. He had to pick a plan and stick with it. He had to get that nuclear torpedo on the MiG out of the target area of the incoming Royal Navy cruise missile.

Bond turned over the Dunhill lighter and flicked a hidden switch. A tiny LCD began a countdown: 5, 4, 3 . . .

Bond threw the lighter behind a pile of oil drums and ran. The handy "light grenade" that Q had provided him exploded two seconds later, and the entire base was turned into utter chaos.

A Scud missile carrier was just on its way past him. It was a lorry with eight wheels and a long flatbed, the missile fastened to it at an angle. The driver had reacted quickly and driven off to get the weapon away from the fire. Bond leaped on it just as the automatic radar kicked in and the Gatling guns spun around to face the explosion. A hail of bullets poured into the area of Bond's diversion.

He heard Tanner urge him on in the headset, "Get out of it, James!"

Now the entire encampment was in a frenzy. Guards, buyers, and sellers were now running about firing aimlessly at unseen enemies. No one noticed the man clinging to the side of the Scud missile carrier as it zoomed past them.

Henry Gupta, in the meantime, clutched the little red box he had paid so much money for. He looked around furiously for his bodyguards. Where the hell were they? He had waited a long time to get his hands on the device. He didn't want the entire operation blown now.

Bond pulled another device from his pack and slapped it onto the side of the Scud carrier. He held onto the vehicle as long as it took to get him to the MiGs, then he dropped to the ground and rolled.

Seconds later, the device exploded, setting off the Scud missile. The flames started spreading, and it wouldn't be long before the fire engulfed the entire secret base.

Two of Gupta's bodyguards jumped onto a moving jeep and commandeered the vehicle by throwing out its driver and passenger. They then spun it around and drove back to their employer. Gupta, perturbed that it had taken the idiots as long as it had, climbed into the jeep.

"Get the hell out of here!" he shouted. The vehicle sped toward the road, leaving the manic confusion behind.

With roughly two minutes until the Navy missile reached its destination, Bond rolled under the closest MiG, the one armed with the nuclear weapon. The pilot, who was standing beneath the aircraft inspecting several bullet holes, turned a moment too late. Bond knocked his feet out from under him, then sprung upright and kicked the pilot in the head. Without stopping to think, he grabbed a helmet, climbed up into the MiG and leaped into the cockpit. The copilot, sitting in the seat behind Bond, shouted at the intruder. He drew a Makarov pistol and pulled the trigger just as Bond slammed a helmet into his nose. The bullet strayed to the right. The man collapsed in his seat, slumping forward.

Bond snapped on the helmet and took a quick look at

the control panel to familiarize himself once again with the cockpit of a MiG-29. He had passed the training course in the early eighties with flying colours, but that had been some time ago. In three seconds, it all came flashing back to him. The fulcrum had a range of 715 miles and could carry a full load of missiles, rockets, or bombs for attacking ground targets. It had a gun in the wing, where it blended into the fuselage. It also possessed what engineers labeled a "look-down/shoot-down" radar, enabling it to look down at low-flying aircraft or missiles. Its top speed was stated to be 1,450 miles per hour and it could reach a height of 50,000 feet in one minute. Bond hoped that statistic was accurate. He fired up the engines and pressed the control to close the double canopy.

Some fifty feet away, the pilot of the second MiG watched in fascination. The bastard was actually stealing a MiG! This was going to be fun . . . !

The engines on the second MiG fired up.

Bond taxied out toward the makeshift runway as some of the terrorists realized what was happening. They turned to fire at the MiG.

Bond spun the plane around so that the jet blast swept across the jeeps and terrorists, brushing them away like flies. He then used the guns under the wings to destroy several dumps of ammunition and rockets. This created a virtual wall of flame and heat. That would keep them away from him long enough to get down the runway.

Bond turned the plane again and barreled out onto the runway at full speed. He took a moment to look up at the sky, estimating that he should be able to see the missile any second.

Sure enough, the cruise missile appeared out of the

13

clouds ahead, coming straight for him. Timing was critical. Bond held the throttles just long enough for the missile to pass directly over him, practically parting his hair, then he shoved the controls forward. The MiG's wheels lifted off the ground just as the missile made impact.

Back in the situation room, the past two minutes had been silent and tense. The observers watched the monitor virtually without breathing. The camera had not moved from the static scene, but the MiG did leave the frame. Not being able to keep their eyes on the nuclear torpedo attached to the MiG's wing, the elite members of Britain's military and intelligence forces could only pray and wait. They heard the drone of the firing officer as he counted down to the moment of impact. They watched as the entire scene on the monitor suddenly blew up spectacularly—then the image on all the screens became video snow.

Back at the site, the impact of the cruise missile had created a hell on earth. The raging fireball that grew into a dome shape over the landing strip threatened to overtake Bond's MiG as he climbed higher and higher. He pushed the throttles as far as they would go and he felt a rare exhilaration as the plane ultimately burst out of the flames into the clear sky.

Bond breathed a sigh of relief. His heart was pounding and the adrenaline was pumping. He had done it. He had got the Soviet torpedo out of there. Damn that admiral . . . Now, the big question was where to go . . . He didn't particularly relish the thought of flying all the way out to HMS *Chester*. He knew of a good restaurant in Peshawar . . . and the woman who managed it was a bit of a morsel herself . . .

The sound of tracers hitting his plane jarred Bond back to his immediate airspace. The second MiG had taken off after him and was now on his tail. A barrage of metal shot out from its guns just as Bond maneuvered evasively to the right. He pulled to the left, then right again, dodging the surprisingly accurate shots of the second pilot.

If that wasn't enough to distract Bond, the copilot behind him began to gain consciousness. It took him a moment to realize what was happening, then he attacked 007 with full force. He pulled a metal lanyard around the intruder's neck and tightened his grip. Bond, gasping for air, heard a thin, high-pitched tone. It could only mean one thing—the MiG in pursuit had fired its heat-seeking missiles at him.

Fighting the garrote, Bond kicked the throttles forward and pulled on the yoke. The MiG went into a spine-crushing turn as the missiles flashed by. Now, if he could just get the plane where he wanted it before the man behind him strangled him to death . . .

The pilot of the MiG in pursuit of Bond cursed when the missile soared past his target. He blinked and saw that the plane had completely disappeared from his view. The thief wasn't in front, nor to the left or right. Where the hell did he go?

Unbeknownst to the second pilot, Bond had managed to position his plane directly underneath his pursuer and keep a comparable speed. Now he strained against the painful vice at his neck as he reached for the red button marked "Copilot Ejector Seat." Finally, after stretching as far as he could tolerate, he tapped it.

The back half of the canopy blew away and the surprised copilot shot up into space. He crashed into the belly of the other MiG, shooting upwards through its bowels until his body erupted into that plane's copilot's seat. The pilot turned around, unable to believe his eyes.

It was the last thing he saw, for the human missile had fatally disabled the plane. The MiG exploded into a thousand pieces.

Bond kicked the throttle of his own MiG forward and muttered, "Backseat driver."

He set a course, put the MiG on afterburners, and settled in. He then reached for the controls of the radio and began to speak into his headset.

"White Knight to Black Rook—"

Back in the situation room, Tanner pulled the plug on the headset so that Bond's voice was transmitted on the speaker for all to hear.

"—returning to castle. And you can tell the Black King that the White Knight would like to shove the whole chessboard right up his bishop."

Admiral Roebuck's face reddened as the others stifled laughter. Even M, who had remained calm and collected throughout the entire ordeal, permitted herself a smile.

Shadow on the Sea

The space around the earth is filled with an abundance of satellites, all circling the globe performing different functions and responsibilities. The principal types are those used for communications purposes, navigational aids, intelligence-gathering, military reconnaissance, and weather tracking. Each satellite is owned by a particular nation, and sometimes by a corporation that in many ways could be more powerful than a country.

The world's business and all news reporting depend upon communications satellites, for without them modern civilization would be crippled. They provide the worldwide linkup of radio and television transmissions, as well as telephone services. After the first satellites were launched in the fifties and early sixties, the International Telecommunications Satellite Organization grew and successfully brought people all over the world closer together. Without the satellites, there would have been no live, televised footage of the Gulf War. There would be no instant replays from sports events taking place in another part of the world.

The progress in communications technology over the last thirty years also improved political relations on the globe. Thanks to the use of satellites, the people of one country could look into a different culture in another hemisphere. Walls were shattered and barriers were crossed. Without the satellites, there would still be fear of another country's military power, their political intentions, and their first strike capabilities.

Several such communications satellites were owned by the massive conglomerate known the world over by the initials CMGN. The Carver Media Group Network was the second largest global news organization, closely rivaling CNN for the number one spot. Everyone in the world knew of CMGN—after all, they had been breaking records in reporting the news faster than any other network. Their slogan, "Tomorrow's News, Today" was becoming more of a reality as CMGN seemed to be everywhere, in every corner of the globe. Even people from countries who were not normally friendly to the West would stop and smile for a CMGN camera. They would be happy to tell the world their philosophy of life, their complaints against capitalism, or make their demands in the latest hostage situation.

One synchronous-orbit CMGN communications satellite was currently directly over southeast Asia, looking down at a drama unfolding in the waters off the coast of China.

The moonlight illuminated the South China Sea with a pale, ghostly effect that made everything lose its colour.

The contrast was such that they might have been the players in a black-and-white film. There was something about sailing on the sea at night that had a calming effect on most travelers. Lovers on a cruise ship, for example, might be lounging on a deck admiring the night sky with their arms around each other. Fishermen might be falling asleep with their pole in hand. Under normal circumstances, most human beings would be lulled to dreamland by the still waters and lack of wind.

Unfortunately, the men aboard HMS *Devonshire* were not enjoying the relative tranquillity of the sea or the moonlight. They were on full alert.

The type 23 Duke class frigate was on routine patrol sailing from the Philippines to Hong Kong when two Chinese MiG-21s zoomed past the ship from stern to bow. The incoming signals from the Chinese were perplexing.

Commander Richard Day, the *Devonshire*'s captain, hurried onto the bridge to join his first officer, Lieutenant Commander Peter Hume.

"Maximum revs, come to 127 degrees," Commander Day ordered.

"I don't understand it, sir," Lieutenant Commander Hume said. "They say we're in Chinese waters. We're too far out to be in Chinese waters!"

Ships at sea depend on another type of satellite for help in navigating the waters of the globe. Navigation satellites launched in 1989 with the NAVSTAR Global Positioning System broadcast time and position messages continuously. Twenty-two NAVSTAR satellites are in use around the earth and are precise to within a few feet for military uses and approximately three hundred feet for nonmilitary uses. There could be no doubt as to the *Devonshire*'s position on the map as indicated by the signal from NAVSTAR.

A yeoman handed Commander Day another Chinese communication. He looked at it and said, "Are they insane? They want us to— Action stations!"

Hume acknowledged the order. "Action stations, sir." He pressed a button and the action stations klaxon began to sound.

Day turned to the yeoman. "Yeoman, send this reply to the Chinese authorities: 'This is the British frigate *Devonshire*. We are not in the position you stated. We are in international waters, seventy-five miles from your coast. We will not go to a Chinese port. You are in violation of international law.'"

The yeoman went on his way and Day picked up the phone to the operations room. "Are we absolutely sure of our position?"

The principal warfare officer in the operations room checked a display showing the three satellite fixes in wide, medium, and close-up views. These things never lied . . . did they?

"Yes, sir," the PWO replied. "An exact satellite fix."

Day muttered, "Go to a Chinese port, indeed . . . Who do they think they are, bullying us like that? Just because they've taken over Hong Kong they think they own the Eastern Hemisphere . . ."

Commander Day was forty-four and had been in the Royal Navy for over twenty years. He knew his way around a ship, and he also had a good understanding of the political complexities of the Far East. He spoke several Oriental languages and had been stationed in Hong Kong for half of his naval career. The Chinese could be very stubborn, and he wasn't about to let them push him around.

The *Devonshire* sped through the sea, but the two MiGs flashed past it once again. The Chinese pilots were receiving orders from their base. From their point of view, the British couldn't possibly expect them to believe what they were claiming. The British Navy was obviously on some sort of spy mission.

On the bridge of the *Devonshire*, the yeoman called out, "Sir, the Chinese signal says their pilot insists we are only eleven miles off their coast, inside their territorial waters, and he'll fire if we don't turn around and go to a Chinese port."

Completely frustrated, Commander Day said, "Send this: 'We are in international waters and will defend ourselves if attacked.' Copy all this to the Admiralty. Urgent."

As the frigate chopped through the waters at full speed, no one noticed the dark, shadowy shape following the British warship. No one could see it, of course, because it was a stealth ship of the latest technology. Consisting of twin hulls, huge pontoons, and strange smooth planes, and painted completely black, the stealth boat was like a creature from the deep that could hide and ambush its prey whenever she felt like it. The bulk of the ship was suspended low over the water by the two pontoons. The area in between was open and covered by the bottom of the ship, allowing the entrance and exit of smaller craft.

There weren't many ships built with stealth technology, certainly not one as custom-made as this one. Uniquely shaped like a gigantic manta ray without a tail, the ship's wide, low profile reduced detection by enemy radar. The ship's surfaces were made of radar-opaque composites and were coated with a radar-absorbing material. Any radar hitting the ship would not be reflected back unless there were a breach in the hull of the ship.

Doors opened beneath the ship's suspended body, in the area between the pontoons. A device known as a Sea-Vac emerged and lowered toward the water. After it submerged, the Sea-Vac snaked quickly toward the *Devonshire*. Technically, it was a jet engine–sized drilling machine equipped with a gleaming set of rotary cutters for teeth and a video camera for an eye. The cutters were three interlocking heads that worked in gear-like fashion. Directional nozzles in the back spewed out water generated by the turbines located in the center of the contraption. It was wire-guided like a modern torpedo. The Sea-Vac was strangely phallic, a probe primed to invade and explore another sea traveler's body.

On the bridge of the stealth ship, a German named Stamper watched the monitors as the Sea-Vac whirred to life. The cutters spun and the intakes howled. As it streaked away toward the British ship, the wire was unspooled behind it. Stamper was pleased. So far, so good. If this went as planned, he would receive a hefty bonus, and perhaps a subject with which to make one of his infamous videotapes. The boss loved his videotapes. The last one he made, with the Filipino girl, was an instant classic. Too bad the tapes couldn't be marketed to connoisseurs of violent pornography. The tapes he made ended up being a little *too* violent.

The thirty-five-year-old German was tall and physically fit. His overall appearance was unsettling, and not because he was unattractive. On the contrary, he had blond hair, blue eyes, broad shoulders, and a body women might die for. What was disturbing was that singular glint behind his piercing blue eyes that suggested there was a screw loose somewhere inside his head.

Stamper thought he would recommend to the boss that the captain of the *Sea Dolphin II* should be replaced. The captain was too nervous for his taste. He liked men to be confident and fearless. The captain kept glancing back at him from the controls, probably fearful that Stamper might put a pistol to his head if he did the wrong thing. Everyone was afraid of him, he knew that. The crew, made up of Germans, Chinese, and a couple of Vietnamese men, obeyed his every command.

Stamper enjoyed his role as the strongman of the organization. He loved to get his hands dirty and play rough. This penchant for violence once got him a prison term of eight years. A further rape charge was tried after Stamper was already in jail, and he was sentenced to another twenty years. If it hadn't been for the boss, he'd still be in there, rotting away with the losers. Stamper wasn't a loser. He won every fight he got into. He could easily take whatever pain and suffering anyone could inflict on him, and then retaliate with the strength of a tiger. To him, it wasn't pain and suffering. It was ecstasy.

Back in the operations room of the *Devonshire,* the men were scurrying to and fro. They had picked up the Sea-Vac on radar but had identified it incorrectly.

"Sir!" the leading seaman shouted to Commander Day and Lieutenant Commander Hume as they rushed into the room. "Torpedo bearing 114, range 8000."

"Alter to 114!" Day responded.

The PWO looked confused as he scanned the radar.

"There's nothing on the surface, sir." It was true: they couldn't see anything on the scanner within miles of their ship.

Hume said, "The MiGs must have dropped it."

The *Devonshire* made a sharp turn in the water, but the Sea-Vac continued to plow ahead, shifting course along with the frigate. The device sped closer and closer to the hull of the ship.

"The torpedo shifted course with us!" the leading seaman reported.

The PWO shouted, "Brace for impact!"

Everyone held his breath for two seconds.

The Sea-Vac struck the ship hard, and the jolt was felt all over the *Devonshire*. In the generator room below, the engineers were knocked to the floor. They looked up at the wall and saw it shudder. Then, a thin circle appeared with a stream trickling through, just before the Sea-Vac burst into the room followed by a torrent of water.

The emergency lighting came on as the main power died in the operations room. Hume reported, "Generators are down, sir. Flooding on C-deck."

"We're down by the stern, sir," the leading seaman added.

The entire ship came alive in an effort to secure the situation. Seamen battened down equipment in the mess room while other crew members ran through to their action stations. The mess room was the next to go, however, for the Sea-Vac exploded through the floor, followed by a geyser of water.

On B-deck above, crew members rushed to close watertight hatches dividing the long corridor while others ran up ladders from below as the wall of water blasted toward them. They were all too late, for the tsunami struck them with great force, knocking them off their feet and carrying their bodies along with it.

Stamper watched from the stealth ship bridge and smiled. The Chinese MiGs were returning. He waited until they were in the correct position.

"Fire number one!" he shouted. "Fire number two!"

Two small heat-seeking missiles streaked up from the deck of the stealth boat toward the two planes. The Chinese pilots shouted a radio message to their base as the sound of the missile lock alarm screamed in their ears. They did their best to maneuver the planes out of harm's way, but the heat-seeking missiles plunged right into the engines. The two MiGs exploded in the air, sending a pair of fireballs down to the dark sea.

Meanwhile, the *Devonshire*'s operations room was alive with flashing lights, alarms, and urgent intercom broadcasts.

"Propulsion system down, sir, engine room doesn't answer," Hume said.

"Sir, we're down 14 degrees by the stern," the leading seaman reported.

Commander Day took only two seconds to make his decision. "Right. Get the men off the ship."

The ship lurched, but Day braced himself. "Yeoman, send to Admiralty: 'Have been torpedoed by Chinese MiGs. Sinking.' Give our position."

Yeoman nodded. "Sending, sir." His hands flew across the keyboard as Hume shouted, "We're going down!"

Then the lights went out.

The *Devonshire*'s stern submerged as her bow rose from the sea. The men donned life jackets and jumped into the cold water. There was no time to activate the life rafts. The ship was sinking faster than anyone had dreamed possible.

Commander Day oversaw evacuation as long as he could, then strapped on a life jacket and followed his men into the water.

Five minutes later, all that was left on the surface was an oil slick and a pitifully small group of Royal Navy sailors paddling helplessly in the water. They thought they were all alone and would probably die quickly so far from land. The moon shone down on them, illuminating their faces of despair as they realized their fate.

When the black shadow moved across their heads, blocking the moonlight, they didn't know what to think. They looked up and gasped at the hulking, dark shape above them. The *Sea Dolphin II* had positioned herself over them so that they were swimming in the area between the two pontoons.

Stamper had made his way to the portside pontoon of the stealth ship and slammed the breech of a large belt-fed machine gun. A crew member with a camcorder stood next to him, training its lens on the British sailors floundering in the water. The German took a moment to savor the feeling of anticipation before pulling the trigger. Then he opened fire, panning the area in front of the ship. The helpless seamen were slaughtered in less than a minute. The entire massacre was caught on videotape by the camcorder.

Had the bullet-riddled sailors sunk to the bottom of the sea, they would have passed the six divers who had emerged from the hull of the stealth ship. They carried a number of tools and underwater torches for illumination. One man carried an underwater video camera. Only one of the divers was armed. They didn't expect to encounter anything hostile now.

The divers swam along the Sea-Vac's wire to the *Devonshire,* which had settled with a thud on the ocean floor near a deep crevasse. The dark hulk was totally without light or life. It might have been the crest of a mountain, buried deep under the sea. One at a time, the divers swam through the hole in the ship's hull, allowing the Sea-Vac's line to lead them to their destination.

Through the maze of rubble and destruction, they swam until the leader held up his hand. He motioned to the others to follow him through a door into a large room full of large and long, dark objects. The leader shone his torch on the objects. He nodded to his companions and motioned for one of them to do his job.

A diver sparked an acetylene torch and went to work on the launch pad clamps securing one of the seven surface-to-surface cruise missiles that the *Devonshire* carried. The torch cut through the metal with ease.

In fifteen minutes, it was all over. The six divers left the hulk and swam back to the stealth ship, carrying the cruise missile. As soon as they were clear, the line on the Sea-Vac went taut. The machine slowly pulled itself out of the rubble-lined tunnel it had carved. The shadowy ship was withdrawing its probe.

In the dark waters beneath the southeast Asian night sky, the entire incident might have looked like a rape—a sexually violent act between two giant sea creatures.

The moonlight did little to illuminate Hamburg, for the city managed to generate an abundance of radiance on its own. Its well-lit skyscrapers were a testament to how, in the last fifty years, the city had become Germany's

27

largest and busiest port. Rebuilt after World War II into a modern cultural centre, Hamburg had long since progressed beyond its reputation as a rough sailor's town and the place where the Beatles paid their dues in the late fifties and early sixties before becoming superstars. Located in the north on the Elbe and Alster rivers, Hamburg is a city of beauty, history, and commerce. It was only natural that the Carver Media Group Network had moved its Western Hemisphere headquarters from London to Hamburg, and rebuilt its Eastern Hemisphere headquarters in Saigon after the Chinese took control of Hong Kong on July 1, 1997.

The new CMGN complex was not yet open to the public. The grand opening ceremony was scheduled to take place the next evening. For days, employees had been scrambling to prepare the building for the grand ribbon-cutting party. All of the world's media would be there, along with many celebrities, dignitaries, and royalty. The floors were still being polished, paint was drying, food was being prepared, and furniture was being arranged. It was an important occasion, for behind the front of the crescent-shaped brick building was an enormous media complex. It was the hub and brain of CMGN's global web of communications.

Since it was just after midnight, many of the workers had called it a day and gone home. Only a few dedicated employees were going about their business scattered in different areas of the building. No one was aware that two men were inside the vast, round control room that was the showpiece of the complex. The newsroom was mostly dark; only a couple of consoles were in use. Incongruously, an enormous red ribbon stretched across the room, awaiting the moment when Elliot Carver would officially open the new headquarters in front of hundreds of people the next evening.

Carver stood at one of the consoles now, weary and exhausted from the thousands of preparations he had been forced to make himself because he trusted few people with the responsibility. At the same time, however, he was anxious and wide awake as he watched the monitors in front of him.

Henry Gupta, a man he had secretly placed on his payroll, sat at one of the consoles manipulating the controls. Gupta's reputation preceded him—Carver had needed no references from the man. Henry Gupta was the world's most accomplished techno-terrorist. There was nothing he couldn't do when it came to electronics. Carver would have liked to have employed him in CMGN's legitimate business if it hadn't been for Gupta's criminal record. He was thus forced to keep Gupta in the background, well hidden and safe.

Elliot Carver was a tall, distinguished-looking man. He had turned fifty recently, was remarkably fit, and carried himself with the authority of aristocracy. A thin man with a receding hairline, Carver possessed a charisma that captivated people around him. He had a commanding presence; when he spoke, others listened. Before he started losing his snow-white hair, Carver had been considered extremely handsome. He still cut a striking figure; his looks and velvet voice had secured him employment as a television anchor when he was young. His interest in media communications grew and, thirty years later, he was the master of all . . . this.

He was proud of his rise to fame and fortune, for he was dealt a bad hand when he first started out in the world a half century ago. He was the illegitimate son of a lord, which, of course, made him heir to nothing. He had never known his German mother, a prostitute. She had died bringing him into the world. Carver was raised by a poor Chinese family in Hong Kong. It was only with a ruthless determination that he was able to leave behind his humble beginnings, become a television anchor in Hong Kong, make a name for himself as a newsman, and eventually inherit his father's vast newspaper empire. There had been some speculation that the lord's suicide was somehow connected to Carver's gain, but no one could prove it.

One thing had led to another and Carver proved to be a shrewd businessman and entrepreneur. He had the foresight to invest in NAVSTAR's Global Positioning System, the GPS, and made a fortune when it became the standard for satellite navigation. His engineers brought new technology to communications satellites, and CMGN was among the first news networks to transmit live coverage of the Gulf War. In a few short years, Elliot Carver had built an empire that spanned the globe.

And that was only the beginning.

His only physical problem, as far as he could tell, was the painful TMJ—temporomandibular joint syndrome— that he experienced whenever he was tense about something. His jaw muscles ached and he heard a clicking sound and felt a grating sensation whenever he opened his mouth wide or chewed his food. His doctor had told him it was due to clenching and grinding his teeth in his sleep—another symptom of too much stress. The doctor prescribed that Carver wear a plastic guard on his upper teeth at night, but he was loath to do that. As he had always been a bit of a martyr, Carver stopped seeing the doctor and went on with his life in chronic pain.

Henry Gupta punched the buttons under the three monitors in front of him. On one of them, the face of Stamper, the German, appeared. He was aboard the stealth ship in the South China Sea.

"It's all done," Stamper said to the camera. "I haven't seen the tape yet, but I'm told it was wonderful through the viewfinder."

The second monitor showed footage of the six divers swimming toward the wreck of the *Devonshire*. Even Carver was impressed by the quality of the tape. The lighting was excellent, almost as if a movie studio had set up the shot with expensive underwater filming equipment. The third monitor snapped on, revealing the start of the tape of the sailors being machine-gunned in the water.

Stamper continued, "It's maybe a little too green, but otherwise it came out very well—look at that one, trying to get away! Got him! Ha ha ha!"

Carver thought that Stamper enjoyed his work far too much, but he was a valuable employee.

Carver and Gupta watched the entire footage on the two screens. They saw the divers enter the wreckage and pull out one of the seven cruise missiles. They watched the British sailors die, one by one. It was perfect.

Carver spoke into a microphone. "Good work, Stamper. We got it all. Now get some sleep, if you can."

Stamper laughed. "Sleep? Are you kidding? After a night like this, I'm ready to party! Ha ha ha!"

Carver shuddered as he imagined how Stamper might spend his time "partying." It was said that when Stamper had a party, there were often several mutilated bodies left in its wake.

"You want a videotape of the party, Boss?" Stamper asked.

"Not this time, Stamper," Carver said.

Gupta moved to another console marked "Satellite Uplink/Downlink." He sat down and carefully unplugged a ruler-size rectangular device from the control panel. It was small enough to fit into the palm of his hand. He then placed the device carefully in the oblong red box he had purchased at the Khyber Pass weapons exchange.

Gupta stood and walked over to Carver. His boss was staring at the blank monitors, contemplating what he had just witnessed.

"So hey!" Gupta said jovially. "What did I tell you? Huh? Am I a genius?"

Carver gestured to the red box and said, "Put that in a safe place. And clean up that console. I don't want any sign that anyone's been in here." Gupta had left a soft drink can and a bag of crisps at his station. Carver wanted to call him a "slob."

"How come? I mean, if anybody has a right to be here—"

Carver cut him off with a sharp look. Gupta knew that look. Elliot Carver was famous among his employees for having "the look." When Elliot Carver gave someone "the look," the boss was *not* to be questioned.

"Okay, okay," Gupta said. "I'll clean up." Offended a little, Gupta turned to do as he was told.

Carver spoke into the microphone and addressed his man in the field again. "Stamper! Play the tape again."

He watched, transfixed, as the the machine gun killed the Royal Navy sailors. Carver asked Stamper to play it yet again in slow motion.

Only then did Carver turn to Gupta and say, "You *are* a genius."

Gupta smiled. His boss was pleased.

THREE

Wai Lin

Exactly forty-eight hours earlier, a jeep had pulled up to the guardhouse of a military encampment just outside Beijing. A Chinese military policeman checked the identification of the driver and his passenger, a woman. Everything was in order. The jeep was ushered through.

Wai Lin squinted as the vehicle drove past barracks and training obstacle courses toward the compound's administration buildings. The sun was very bright today. She reached into her handbag, pulled out a pair of sunglasses, and put them on.

The jeep soon stopped in front of the main administrative building. Wai Lin told the driver in Mandarin to wait there. She was fluent in nearly all of the Chinese dialects. She had grown up with Cantonese as her primary tongue, but as her career moved her into political and military arenas, Mandarin became more important.

She stepped out of the jeep. An MP admired her looks

from the front door, although he pretended to be at attention. Wai Lin knew she was attractive, even in the stiff uniform of the Chinese army. Small in stature, like most Chinese women, she managed to look taller in the military fatigues. Perhaps it was the air of authority that she naturally carried. It suited her for the line of work she was in.

She had long black hair parted in the middle that came down just past her shoulder blades. Her almond-shaped brown eyes were set wide apart on an oval face. Her mouth was small and delicate, but she had a smile that could melt hearts. She was thin but shapely. Underneath the uniform her body was muscular and well toned. Her breasts were the size of small apples, but they were firm and well proportioned to the rest of her figure. Her former fiancé had always said her breasts were "perfect."

Wai Lin had often got the impression that she was too strong and threatening for men. Her love life had suffered because she was the type of woman who enjoyed being the aggressor. In China, that was not the norm. Women were supposed to be subservient and passive. Not Wai Lin. The last time she allowed a man to be the dominant partner in a relationship, it ended with her losing her temper and humiliating the man. He picked up his things and left their little flat in Shanghai. They were supposed to have been married in a week. With hindsight, she was glad it fell through. Wai Lin couldn't imagine being married now. Her career had taken off, and she found more satisfaction in her work than anything else that had occupied her twenty-eight years of life on the planet.

Wai Lin removed her sunglasses, returned the MP's salute, and went inside the building. She showed her pass to the officer behind the counter, then another MP led her through a door and down a hallway.

When they went through another door, it became obvious that something had happened in the building. Several MPs were stationed along the new hallway, and there was a flurry of activity in the office at the end of the corridor. Wai Lin was led into the room, where soldiers were dismantling furniture, going through files, and examining the walls and windows.

The MP approached a general standing in the middle of the room overseeing the operation. The general turned and looked at Wai Lin. She saluted and the MP introduced her as "Colonel Lin." The general's name was Koh.

"Welcome, Colonel," the general said in Mandarin. "It's nice to see you again. We have much to discuss. As you can see, we are dismantling the traitor's office now. So far we have not found anything. Come with me."

She followed him out of the room and down the hall to a temporary office. General Koh gestured for her to sit.

"Colonel, you have been briefed by your superiors in Beijing?" he asked.

"Of course, sir," she said.

"What do you know?"

"General Chang has disappeared. It is believed he has taken some vital secrets with him."

"You are aware of what secrets we believe he has stolen?"

"Yes," she replied. "The Russian low-emission radar technology."

"You understand the implications?"

"The low-emission radar produces such low-frequency waves that a stealth plane could use it without giving itself away. Our government obtained one of the devices a month ago during a reconnaissance mission in Irkutsk. General Chang was put in charge of its safekeeping."

"The use of that radar in our own stealth vehicles would have boosted our military capabilities. We would be on the same level as the Americans and Russians. It's important that we get it back."

"Do we have any idea where General Chang might be now?"

"Not yet," Koh said. "According to statements given to me by his staff—which we had to forcefully extract from them—General Chang left the base two days ago and flew to Vietnam. It's possible that he's still there, since our agents have been combing the airport and train stations. He may be well disguised, or he's hiding somewhere until he thinks it's safe to leave."

"Was the device with him when he left?"

"No," Koh said. "We believe it went ahead of him, and probably not to the same destination. He couldn't very well travel with it. According to his second-in-command, the radar was packed in a crate full of straw and labeled as tea two to three weeks ago. We're trying to trace the shipment now."

"I presume you want me to go to Vietnam and look for him?" she asked.

"No. I want you to trace the shipment of tea. General Chang is not the most important thing here, the radar is. After we find the radar, then we'll deal with the traitor."

General Koh placed a stack of papers on the edge of the desk. "Here is all the relevant information. Maybe you can find a clue with that keen eye of yours."

It was the first compliment the general had ever given her.

"I shall do my best, sir," she said.

The general smiled. "You look pretty good in that uniform, Miss Lin. Maybe you should leave the People's External Security Force and join the Army!"

She glanced up at him. "No, thank you, sir. I'm quite content to wear the uniform for reasons of cover."

"Well, you look very natural in it. That's good. We don't want the men here to get the idea that the Chinese Secret Service is looking for their general. It wouldn't help morale."

"Will that be all?" she asked.

"For now. Let me know what you find." With that, the general left the room. Wai Lin started examining the documents, one by one.

Beijing, formerly known in the West as Peking, is administered directly by the central government. As the second largest city in China after Shanghai, Beijing enjoys its status as the political, financial, educational, and transportation center of the country. Since the advent of the People's Republic of China, the city had become a major industrial area. Much of the industry is located on the outer edges of the city, away from the tourist areas of the Forbidden City, the Gate of Heavenly Peace, Tiananmen Square, the national library, and the world famous zoo.

Wai Lin found the Xiang Warehouse in this area of industrial commerce. She parked her modest Toyota Camry away from the floodlights illuminating the parking lot and stepped out onto the pavement. She was now dressed in civilian clothes: a sharp black trouser suit with a red waistcoat.

It was after hours, and the warehouse was closed. The

workers had gone home for the day, but Wai Lin was taking no chances. She moved cautiously around the building to the back, where a door marked in Chinese characters read: "Employee Entrance." It was locked, of course, but that didn't stop her. She glanced around to make sure no one was looking, then used a concealed lockpick to gain entrance to the building.

The large warehouse was dark, lit only by a couple of work lights left on overnight. They were sufficient for her to see where she was going, though. The place was full of what appeared to be a combination of automotive parts and produce. She moved stealthily past stacks of crates and boxes toward the front office. She stopped when she heard a couple of voices in the distance—the night guards, most likely.

Wai Lin peered around a column of tires and saw them. They were smoking cigarettes, standing in front of the main office. The men were armed with what looked like Chinese copies of Makarov pistols. The lights were on inside the office, which could be seen through the plate-glass window in the wall behind the security guards.

She turned away and moved back down the aisle so that she could approach them from a different angle. She passed another tower of tyres and got an idea.

The two guards were telling off-colour jokes and laughing. Never in a million years did they think their services would ever really be needed at the warehouse. It was an easy job. They had never had to use their guns, and probably never would. Who would want to steal anything from this place? There was nothing here but junky car parts and rotting vegetables.

The laughter subsided and one guard sighed. He couldn't think of another joke.

"You have another cigarette?" he asked his companion.

As the man reached for his pocket, they both heard a noise down one of the dark aisles.

They stopped and looked at each other.

"Did you hear that?"

The other man nodded. They stood still and listened.

Then, incongruously, a single tyre came rolling slowly out of the darkness down the aisle toward them. They watched in amazement as the tyre slowed to a stop about twenty feet away from them. It then turned and fell to the floor, still rotating, like a coin that had been spun on its side.

The guards immediately drew their pistols and walked over to the tire. One man gestured to the other to go down the aisle.

He walked cautiously into the dark aisle past the rows of stacked crates and tyres. The light was very dim in this section of the warehouse. He held his pistol nervously, wondering who could be playing such a trick on them. When he was forty feet away from the office and his partner, he came to an intersection of aisles. He looked in both directions, then continued forward.

Wai Lin was silent and quick. She stepped out from behind a column of crates and moved up to the guard. One lightning chop on the back of his neck with her spear-shaped hand sent the man to his knees. She quickly covered his mouth with her other hand, then hit him one more time to knock him out.

The first guard called, "Hey! Find anything?"

It was too quiet.

"What's going on?" he called. "Answer me, you idiot!"

When there was no reply, the first guard became concerned. With his pistol ready, he began to creep down the aisle in search of his partner.

He found the unconscious guard where Wai Lin had left him, sprawled facedown on the concrete floor. The first guard bent down to examine him. Then he felt the cold muzzle of the Makarov pistol at the back of his head.

"Drop it," Wai Lin said. The guard did as he was told. "Now get up slowly. Don't try anything stupid."

The guard stood up, but unfortunately he tried something stupid. He attempted to twist around and grab Wai Lin's gun and use an inept karate throw to disarm her. The woman's experience far exceeded the guard's. Not only did she block his attack, but she sent him hurling over her head into the stack of tires, knocking them to the floor. She pointed the gun at him again.

"All right, we'll try one more time," she said. "Get up slowly. And if you do something like that again, I won't be so easy on you."

The guard nodded and was completely under her control.

She forced him to open the office door with his keys, then told him to get her all the shipping records for the warehouse for the past month.

"Now, be a good boy and sit on the floor facing the wall there. Keep your hands on your head while I look at these," she said. "If you move, I'll just have to hurt you. Don't worry about your friend. He'll be fine. It was a nerve chop. He'll be out for an hour and wake up with a splitting headache."

Once the guard was in position, Wai Lin started examining the records. She finally found a shipment of tea that had left the warehouse two-and-a-half weeks ago. There was a cross-reference to another book that indicated where the tea went. She looked for the book but couldn't find it.

"Where's the client log?" she asked the guard.

He replied that he didn't know.

She moved to him and took his right earlobe between her thumb and index finger.

"Are you sure?" she asked again.

When he nodded hesitantly, she knew he was lying. She pinched him hard. He yelled, then capitulated. "All right! All right! The manager . . . Mr. Deng, he has it. He keeps it at his flat."

"How do you know that?"

"He told me! He says he keeps the most important records there."

Probably because he's involved in criminal activity, she thought.

"All right, where do I find this Mr. Deng?" she asked.

"Now? He won't be home . . ."

"Where would he be?"

"Well . . ." When the guard told her, she laughed and shook her head.

The black limousine pulled up along the busy street full of nightclubs and streetwalkers and stopped where Wai Lin stood in a long, slinky red *cheongsam* with one shapely leg seductively sticking out of the slit. The automatic window lowered and the Chinese man in the backseat called to her.

"How much to spend the night at my place?" he asked her.

Wai Lin pretended to consider the proposition. "Eight thousand yuan," she said. The man raised his eyebrows.

"That's expensive!"

"I'm worth it," she said. "You interested or not?"

The man looked her up and down. "Turn around," he said. Wai Lin did a graceful turn and ended back where she started, only this time more of her leg was revealed.

"All right," he said. "Get in." The door opened and she got in the back with him.

"What's your name?" he asked.

"Anita," she said.

"What's your Chinese name?" he asked.

Wai Lin shook her head. "Just Anita, all right? What do I call you?"

"You can call me Mr. Deng."

The car went about six miles north and ended up in a residential section. The limousine let them out in the underground parking garage of a high-rise apartment building that was occupied by an elite, wealthy clientele.

Wai Lin followed Deng, an overweight man in his forties, into a lift and up to the sixteenth floor. He unlocked the door to his flat and held it open for her. In the brighter light of the hallway, she could see that Deng wore a toupee.

The flat was elegantly furnished, but obviously the home of a bachelor. There were few amenities apart from the colour television and expensive stereo system. Deng asked her to sit down while he made some drinks. Despite living in a Communist country, Mr. Deng had obviously done well for himself. Again, Wai Lin attributed this to criminal activity.

"Um, I need the money before we go any further," she said.

Deng said, "All right, wait there." He went into the bedroom.

Wai Lin looked around the room and noticed a few framed photographs on a bookshelf. She wasn't surprised when she saw a picture of Deng with General Chang standing in front of the Gate of Heavenly Peace. What did astonish her was the photo of the so-called "Crown Prince Hung." Hung looked like a rock star, almost a Chinese version of Michael Jackson—complete with gaudy eyeliner, slick black hair, and lipstick. A few years ago, Hung had created a stir when he announced that he was the true heir of the Ming Dynasty. He even had the audacity to "predict" that he would one day take the throne and bring China back to its former days of glory before the revolution. Hung and his entourage were exiled from the country, and the last Secret Service reports Wai Lin had seen indicated that he was living in Zurich. Wai Lin looked closer at the photo and noticed that some men in military uniforms were in the background. It was impossible to tell where the picture had been taken, but she was positive that she recognized General Chang grinning behind the dubious crown prince. Wai Lin wondered if there was a connection between Chang and Hung.

Deng called to her from the bedroom. "Come in here!"

On her guard, Wai Lin stepped to the doorway and listened. She could hear the man's heavy breathing behind the door. He was most likely planning to surprise her and probably to do something unpleasant to her.

Wai Lin kicked the door hard into Deng, and he let out a howl. She dived into the room and avoided a shot from

Deng's flimsy revolver. She jumped backward, grabbed Deng's right hand, and threw him over her shoulder onto the floor. She picked up his gun and pointed it at him. He was dressed only in boxer shorts.

"Wait, don't shoot!" Deng cried. He looked ridiculously pitiful on the floor.

"You were going to hurt me with this, weren't you?" she said. "You weren't going to pay me, were you?"

Deng just stammered, "No . . . no . . . I . . . er . . . yes . . . I mean . . ."

"Fine," Wai Lin said. She placed one high heel on his bare chest, revealing a smooth leg all the way up to the top of her thigh. "Just tell me what I want to know and I'll forget the whole thing. Where is the client log from the warehouse?"

Deng looked surprised. He had thought he was about to be robbed by a prostitute. "Over there, on the desk!" He pointed to a corner of the room.

She ordered him to stay put, then walked over to the desk. She thumbed through the book until she found the reference number she was looking for. Written neatly in Chinese characters were the words "Three shipments of tea . . . Carver Media Group Network Building . . . Hamburg, Germany."

Wai Lin went back to the blubbering man on the floor. "Where is General Chang?" she asked.

"I don't know!" he said.

She cocked the revolver and pointed it at his forehead.

"Honest!" he cried. "I haven't seen him in over two weeks."

"Did he deliver some crates to you for shipping?"

"Yes, it was tea!"

"That's the last you saw of him?" She shoved the muzzle of the gun a little harder into his forehead.

"I swear!"

Wai Lin was a good judge of people. She had earned extremely high marks in her interrogation courses. Deng was telling the truth. He was too frightened not to.

"Very well. I'm going to keep this gun," she said. "You're going to stay on the floor for ten minutes after I leave. All right?"

"You're . . . you're not going to kill me?" he asked, the sweat pouring down his face.

Wai Lin just smiled sweetly at him.

"And another thing," she said. "If you hear from General Chang at all, you must contact the police. If we learn that you've been talking to him, you will be arrested. Do we understand each other?"

Deng nodded furiously. He was beginning to understand now. The girl was some kind of cop!

Wai Lin got up and backed out of the bedroom.

Deng raised his head and asked, "I guess this means I don't get to see you naked?"

The shot blew the toupee off his head. He screamed and held the top of his head with a look of sheer panic on his face. When he realized he was still alive, he looked at her in horror.

"Maybe next time," Wai Lin said. She blew the smoke away from the gun barrel, turned, and quickly left the flat.

FOUR

Mission Du Jour

J ames Bond had always been a poor student. When he
was a boy, he didn't do well in school. It wasn't that
he didn't have the capacity to perform well; he was
simply bored by it all. A restless soul, Bond was the sort
of man who couldn't stay inactive for any length of time.
The day-in, day-out routine of school quickly grew
tiresome and he needed to move. He was a man of action.

His career at Eton was undistinguished. He spent two
years there, mostly excelling in athletics and ignoring
academics. Then he was caught in that little indiscretion
with one of the boys' maids. He was asked to leave the
school, and he was glad. The "old school tie" never held
much significance for him.

After Eton, Bond went to Fettes, his father's old
school. What interested him was athletics again, history
and military training. He had no more proper schooling
after that. What came next was naval service at a very

young age, followed by induction into the British Secret Service.

Bond once had a bad habit of telling people he had been to Cambridge. He remembered trying to impress Miss Moneypenny by telling her that he took a first in Oriental languages there. It wasn't true. It was the only white lie he ever used to tell, Bond thought to himself with amusement. On second thought, he recalled lying about his age to get into the Royal Navy. And then there were the dozens of excuses he dreamed up to explain to M what he was doing at such-and-such a time.

Since his induction into the Service, Bond had made it a point to educate himself on his own terms. It was on his own initiative that he learned additional foreign languages, other than the German and French he already spoke fluently. He had learned German as a youth, since he spent most of his childhood in Germany with his parents, before they were killed in a climbing accident. He studied chemistry and forensic sciences through courses offered by MI6. As he grew older, he developed the need to read voraciously. He soaked up the details he felt were important to remember and discarded the rest. It was important that every agent, especially a Double-O, keep his mind from rotting away. The latest technology must be constantly studied and analyzed. Knowledge of the world's politics and current affairs was crucial. Therefore, the more languages one knew, the better.

It was for this reason that James Bond awoke early with the intention of traveling up to Oxford in his Aston Martin DB5. A lecturer at Balliol had been teaching him Danish for the past three months. He was due for a lesson.

Bond had a breakfast of very strong coffee from De

Bry in New Oxford Street, a brown egg, from a French Maran hen, boiled for three-and-a-third minutes, and two thick slices of whole wheat toast. He dressed, said good-bye to May, his elderly Scottish housekeeper, and left the flat where he had lived for years. He pulled the DB5 out onto the King's Road, and headed north.

He knew that it was probably a bad idea to take such a classic car out onto English highways, but everyone who owned such a car did so and he still loved to drive it. It had belonged to the Service for years. When Q Branch decided to work with BMW and other automobile manufacturers, some of the company Aston Martins were sold to the highest bidders. Bond had outbid Bill Tanner for the car by five thousand pounds. His personal mechanic, Melvin Heckman, kept it in superb shape and also allowed Bond to store it in a private garage.

The drive to Oxford always went faster than he expected. He surprised the professor by arriving an hour early for his appointment. She had just returned from a morning lecture and was still dressed in her black gown. As usual, Professor Inga Bergstrom made good use of the extra time. She wanted to make sure her favourite pupil got his lessons right.

"I am very pleased with your progress, Mr. Bond," she said in Danish after two hours had elapsed.

"It's all because of you, Professor," he said in perfect Danish, as if he had come from Copenhagen.

"You have a naturally clever tongue," she sighed.

"You inspire me to use it well," he said, then leaned in to kiss her.

The couple had made a mess of the sofa bed in the professor's office. The wild sprawl of sheets was totally out of place amid the framed academic degrees, the neatly filed books on the shelves, and pictures of the beautiful, blue-eyed blond professor in her gown. She was a strong woman, possessing the distinctive large bone structure of the Danes. Bond admired particularly her callipygian posterior. Her maturity, intellect, and voluptuousness combined to make her a highly stimulating teacher. The sofa bed was used by the professor only for difficult cases of tutelage. As it had been two weeks since his last visit, Mr. Bond had a lot of catching up to do. He had managed to show her that he was a fast, but completely thorough, learner.

Totally spent, Bond lit two cigarettes with the distinctive three gold bands and handed one to Professor Bergstrom. Inga sighed heavily and allowed him to place the cigarette between her lips. She took hold of his wrist with her right hand and held the cigarette with her left. Bringing his fingers to her mouth, she started licking and nibbling on them.

"If you're hungry, maybe we should have lunch," he suggested in English.

"Danish, James, Danish. You always take me to ridiculously chic restaurants," she said in her language. "Why don't you let me fix us some sandwiches? Besides, I like the taste of your fingers for now. They make good appetizers."

Bond closed his eyes and allowed her to continue with her oral fixation, but then he heard the faint buzzing sound coming from the pile of clothes on the other side of the room.

"There it is again," she said, in Danish. "Listen. I think there's a bee over there."

Bond shook his head. "Damn. How long has that been going on?"

He slipped out from under the sheet and pulled on his discarded shorts. Inga sat up with a crease in her brow. Bond went over to his suit and reached into the jacket pocket.

"What is it?" Inga asked.

"How do you say 'cell phone' in Danish?" he asked her in her language. He pulled out the antenna and spoke English into the phone, "This is Bond. Going to scrambler channel four."

In London, Miss Moneypenny sat in the Ministry of Defence situation room. Everyone had assembled for the briefing. The staff officers were already calling out reports. M and Bill Tanner stood behind her, impatiently waiting for Bond to arrive so that they could begin. They didn't like to keep the minister of defence, the first lord of the Admiralty, or the first sea lord longer than they had to.

"Where have you been?" Moneypenny whispered, covering her ear so that she could hear him. "I've been trying you for an hour! There's a full alert! Haven't you seen the TV?"

Bond winced. He could hear the staff officers in the background: "Sir, HMS *Invincible* is under way from Gibraltar" . . . "Sir, *Defiant*'s trailing a Chinese sub" . . .

"I haven't seen the TV," Bond said. "I'm at Oxford, being tutored. In fact, I was just at the point of mastering a new tongue."

"Well, you'll be neutered if you don't get here right now," Moneypenny said.

"James!" Professor Bergstrom called a little too loudly. "Come back to bed."

Bond could envision Moneypenny's smirk. "And I suppose that's your professor," she said flatly.

"Yes! She is!"

Moneypenny wasn't putting up with it. "We're at the Ministry of Defence. Turn on the radio on the way. It's a major crisis. We're sending the fleet to China. Be here in ten minutes."

"I'm two hours away," Bond said. "It will take me sixty minutes."

"Where are you?" Moneypenny asked again.

"I told you, in Oxford, in my professor's study."

After a slight pause, Moneypenny said, "I've never heard it called that. 'She lifted her dress to reveal her study.'"

Moneypenny was about to giggle at her own joke, but she looked up and saw M standing above her. She blanched and hung up the phone.

"Don't ask," she said.

"Don't tell," M added.

Bond had understated slightly the amount of time it would take for him to reach the Ministry of Defence Building in Whitehall. The Aston Martin slid into the side street behind the building exactly one hour and twenty minutes after he had rung off with Moneypenny. It still wouldn't be fast enough to suit M, but it was the best he could do. It took another minute for him to stop at the security gate and have a sentry check him through. He parked behind M's Rolls-Royce and hurried into an unmarked rear entrance guarded by more sentries.

The meeting had begun without him. The noise level was high as staff officers transmitted orders and received reports. The wall-sized video screens were full shots of the Royal Navy fleet preparing to set sail for the South China Sea. One monitor displayed the video of Henry Gupta buying the red box at the terrorist swap meet. Bond wasn't surprised to see the decorations on parade in the room. He recognized almost everyone—the first sea lord, and certainly Admiral Roebuck, who was in the middle of what looked like a rumble with none other than M. It was probably a good thing, because his tardiness wasn't noticed.

"You're taking the side of the Chinese Air Force against the Royal Navy!" Roebuck said, his face turning red with frustration.

"That's absurd!" M huffed. She could be extremely tough when she wanted to. Bond's admiration for the woman had increased over the months.

"They sink one of our ships and you want to have a 'joint investigation'? Of all the cowardly—"

"Disagree with me if you like, but say the word 'cowardly' again and I'll invite you to step outside," she said calmly.

Bond glanced at the silent Bill Tanner when the minister of defence entered the room just in time to hear M's last words.

"What's this?" he asked. "M, it almost sounded like you were challenging Admiral Roebuck to a . . . to a fistfight."

"Yes, Minister, I certainly was," she replied.

"We can't have this squabbling, we're in a national crisis!" he declared. "Emergency cabinet meeting in ten minutes—what's the situation?"

The first sea lord piped up. "Admiral Kelly has three frigates there now, another three by tomorrow."

"It wouldn't matter if we had *fifty* there tomorrow, our

ships are ten minutes from the largest Air Force base in China!" M pointed out. "And the Chinese won't let our fleet stay that close. It would be like our having a Chinese fleet in the Channel."

Admiral Roebuck threw up his hands. "So you're saying that if they sink one of our ships, we should just take it?"

"Damn it." M glared at him. "That is not—"

"Please!" the minister shouted. "M, what *are* you saying?"

Roebuck answered for her. "She's saying that the Chinese pilots were right and our ship *was* off course, in spite of the latest satellite navigation systems!"

"I am *saying*," M interjected, "that the GPS system could have been tampered with."

"I thought that was impossible," the minister said.

"Tanner!" M called.

The chief of staff, and longtime friend of Bond, stepped in to help her. "As you know, sir, ships at sea, along with airplanes and even hikers, rely on the Global Positioning Satellite System, the GPS. A network of U.S. Department of Defense satellites broadcast continuous time signals, derived from land-based atomic clocks."

"I do know that," the minister said, "and I have five minutes."

Slightly rattled, Tanner sped up his speech. "These signals are encoded, so that the receiver knows which satellite is broadcasting what signal. The Atomic Clock Signal Encoding System—which the Americans call ACSES—is one of the most carefully guarded U.S. secrets."

As Tanner spoke, a staff officer rushed into the room with a stack of newspapers. He started handing them out.

The minister glanced at his paper in horror as Tanner continued, "There are only twenty-two ACSES devices in the world."

"My God!" the minister said. "This is utterly appalling." He looked at M and handed her his paper. "Excuse me, M. The late edition of *Tomorrow*."

The headline screamed: "BRITISH SAILORS MURDERED—Seventeen Machine-Gunned Bodies Found."

"A Vietnamese fishing boat picked them up," the minister read. "Some of them boys of eighteen."

Roebuck read on. "Riddled by the same type of shells Chinese MiGs use."

The minister looked at the chief of staff and said, sardonically, "Go on, Tanner."

"There was a twenty-third ACSES device, believed lost in the explosion of a U.S. Air Force transport . . ."

Bond, sensing that Tanner was losing his audience to the spectacular headlines in the paper, stepped to the monitor running Gupta's videotape and pressed a button. The frame froze on Gupta holding the red box.

"That's the missing ACSES," he said, loud enough to attract everyone's attention. "And with it, someone technically sophisticated, like the man holding it, could make an ordinary satellite pose as a GPS satellite, and send a ship off course."

Roebuck looked down his nose at the newcomer. "And who are you, sir?"

Bond replied, "I'm White Knight, you're Black King, and I owe you a chessboard."

"What?" the minister asked, totally without a clue.

"Never mind, Minister," M said. "Continue, Tanner."

"One of the CMGN satellites over China—a news satellite that never got permission to broadcast—did send a signal on the night in question."

"So this signal sent the ship off course?" the minister asked.

"M can't say that," Roebuck huffed. "Can you?"

"No," M said self-effacingly. "We only know that it's possible." She looked at Bond and he acknowledged that he agreed with her.

"There's no evidence at all," Roebuck said. "But when our fleet finds the *Devonshire,* we'll have the evidence! Only M says we should not send the fleet, but instead go hat in hand to the Chinese and ask for a 'joint investigation'!"

"Is this true?" the minister asked her.

"I wouldn't say 'hat in hand,' but that's exactly what I recommend," M answered.

"M, really, that's impossible," the Minister said, shaking his head. "The papers are howling for blood! If we did that, the media would have our heads."

"I was just accused of cowardice," M said. "But I'd be happy to stand before the media and tell them all to go to hell before I'd put the country in danger."

The minister's eyes tightened. "Step over here with me, please, M."

He took her out of earshot of the others. Bond and Tanner exchanged glances again and drifted together.

"She's right, but she's gone too far this time," Tanner whispered. "They might make her resign."

"I'll bet you they can't," Bond said.

"Can I have your car keys?"

"I'm not betting my car on it, Bill."

"No, no, I'm having it picked up. You're coming with us."

M finished her private word with the Minister and strode tight-lipped past the admirals, then past Bond and Tanner. They shared another glance, then followed her out of the room.

A police escort led the enormous vintage Rolls-Royce out of the courtyard gates. Inside, M, Tanner, and Bond sat in luxury as the car left Whitehall and headed out of London. Bond sat on the jump seat, facing M and her chief of staff.

Bond studied M's expression as they drove away in silence. M showed no signs of distress over what had just happened in front of her staff in the building. She remained cool and calm, for she was confident that she was right. Bond knew that she would have taken Admiral Roebuck to the cleaners had he accepted her challenge to step outside.

M and Bond had strengthened their relationship since she took over as the head of MI6. At first they had a shaky alliance, but once he had proven himself in the field and shown her that his reputation was not fictional, they got along splendidly. Like her predecessor, Sir Miles Messervy, she disapproved of Bond's womanizing and schoolboy antics, but she knew a good agent when she saw one. She had learned to put up with the flaws in favour of the fortunes.

Tanner poured three glasses of scotch from a crystal decanter as M pressed a button. A panel next to Bond slid back, revealing a sophisticated communications board. She pressed another button and the privacy panel behind Bond's head slid down, revealing Miss Moneypenny, sitting next to the driver. She was equipped with telephones and a laptop computer. Not only did M have a traveling office, Moneypenny had a traveling *outer* office.

"Evening, James," Moneypenny said. Her red hair glistened in the sunlight.

"Evening, Moneypenny," Bond said. He lifted his glass. "*Skoal.*"

"Moneypenny, leak a story to the *Express*," M said. "Say the government would like to sack me, but they are afraid of all my files on everyone."

She addressed Bond and Tanner. "That should buy us a couple of days. But in two days it won't matter who gets fired, we could be in a war we can't possibly win. They're so sure they are right, and they have a great deal of evidence. We have none. Just two or three things that don't fit."

The Rolls made a tight turn through a roundabout. Although the car swayed, M behaved as if it were standing still.

"Sorry about this, but we only have a few minutes to get you to Heathrow," she said to Bond.

These were words 007 loved to hear.

"Beijing, M? Hong Kong again?"

"No. Hamburg. I believe you know the wife of Elliot Carver."

Bond frowned. "Yes. I used to know her very well, when she was Paris McKenna. But very few people know that."

He turned and met Moneypenny's eyes. She shrugged and said, "Queen and country, James."

M scrutinized Bond. "You gave me a look, in there, when Tanner was talking about the satellite. Why?"

"He mentioned a Carver Media Group Network satellite, and it struck me that the *Tomorrow* newspaper also belongs to Elliot Carver."

"Exactly." She was pleased that he was thinking along her lines.

On cue, Tanner handed Bond a thick file. "Elliot Carver, born in Hong Kong, officially an orphan, unofficially the illegitimate son of Lord Roverman, the Hong Kong and London press lord, and a German woman, who died in childbirth. A poor Chinese family agreed to take the boy for a one-time fee of fifty pounds. Thirty years later, Carver was somehow able to acquire the Roverman newspapers, which he folded into *Tomorrow*, and his unofficial father committed suicide."

"And who says that family values are declining today," Bond quipped.

The Rolls pulled onto the motorway toward Heathrow. They would be there in minutes.

"You'll read the rest in the file. It's fascinating," M said.

"You think Carver is involved in this?" Bond asked.

"Just before the CMGN satellite in Asia sent that unknown signal, another unknown signal was beamed from the CMGN broadcast center in Hamburg," said Tanner. "A center which does not open until tonight. Carver's holding a huge reception there."

Moneypenny handed Bond an envelope.

"Your ticket, cover story, and rental car reservation," she said. "Sign there, please."

As Bond officially accepted the documents, M continued, "Carver owns satellites. You saw that terrorist Gupta buy a device that can only be used with a satellite. Your

61

job is to find out if there's a connection. Stir things up with Carver. Use your relationship with Mrs Carver."

"I doubt if she'll even remember me," he said.

"Remind her. Then pump her for information."

Bond handed the signed chit back to Moneypenny, who whispered, "I suppose you'll have to decide how much pumping is needed."

"If only that were true of me and you," he whispered back.

Moneypenny smiled sweetly, then raised the divider. M leaned forward to Bond and said, "You'll read the file. And it will sound as if you're just going to a big party. But if I'm right about this, you'll be in terrible danger."

"I wouldn't have it any other way," Bond said.

By then, the Rolls had made its way through a security gate at Heathrow Airport and driven straight out onto the tarmac. A British Airways 757 was ready to go. Personnel were pushing stairs up to the aircraft as the Rolls pulled in and stopped.

"Be careful, Double-O Seven" was the last thing M said before Bond stepped out of the car.

FIVE

He Who Gets Slapped

The British Airways 757 touched down at Flughafen
Fuhlsbuttel, otherwise known as Airport Hamburg,
on time in the afternoon. The terminal was ultramodern,
sporting a unique passenger pier with a roof shaped like
an enormous aircraft wing.

Bond enjoyed Hamburg and had spent some of his
youth there. He fondly remembered visiting the Reeper-
bahn with some fellow Royal Navy sailors before he
joined the Secret Service. He had been to red light
districts before, especially in Amsterdam, but nothing
compared to what he saw on the Grosse Freiheit, a street
meaning "great freedom." The Herberstrasse, where
working girls displayed their wares in shop windows and
invited visiting sailors inside for a business transaction,
was an eye-opener.

He made his way to the Avis counter, where a pretty
girl greeted him warmly. "Can I help you, sir?" she asked
in German.

"Yes," Bond said, also in German. "My office reserved a car." He handed her the reservation form Moneypenny had given him.

"One moment, please," the girl said, and disappeared.

Bond wondered what kind of car he might get. He knew that Q had been working on a Jaguar XK8 for the past few months, and he was looking forward to test-driving it.

007's training took over, and on reflex he scanned the place for anyone or anything out of the ordinary. As he finished the sweep of the room, his eyes landed on the editions of *Tomorrow* on the newsstand. The headline proclaimed: "CHINA WARNS BRITISH FLEET."

"If you'll just sign *here*, Mr. Bond." It was a voice from behind him that Bond recognized immediately.

He turned to behold the inimitable Q dressed in a red Avis jacket. He looked tired. Bond nearly blew their cover by bursting into laughter.

Q slapped down the reservation form on the counter. "It's the insurance damage waiver, for your *beautiful new car*."

Bond was going to enjoy this. Dear Major Boothroyd, the head of Q Branch and the official armourer for the Secret Service, was probably the only man he would call a genius. If Bond hadn't been so fond of him, he wouldn't torment him so. Q was getting on in years, but he still retained a good deal of spirit. Their byplay had become as familiar as Bond's unstirred, shaken vodka martini.

Through clenched teeth, Q asked questions and checked off the applicable boxes on the form as Bond answered.

"Will you need a collision damage waiver?"

"Yes."

"Fire?"

"Probably."

"Property destruction?"

"Definitely."

"Personal injury?"

"I hope not. But accidents *do* happen."

The major noticed that some civilians waiting in the queue had heard their conversation. He huffed and handed Bond a pen. 007 signed the form.

"Well, that takes care of *normal* wear and tear," Bond said. "Do I need any other protection?"

Q was seething. "Only from me, Double-O Seven," he whispered. He gestured forcefully with head and shoulders, then opened a door behind the counter. Bond went around and followed him inside.

They were in the Customs Holding Area. Two large crates stood on the pavement.

"Now, pay attention, Double-O Seven," Q said. "First, your new car."

Q flipped a latch, and the side of the first crate fell open to reveal an angry jaguar in a cage.

The animal snarled loudly at Bond, scaring the living daylights out of him.

Q laughed aloud. "Wrong assignment! Sorry!"

Bond relaxed and laughed, too.

Q moved on to the other crate, but Bond lingered, looking at the animal.

Still chuckling, Q led Bond to the other crate. He was terribly pleased with his practical joke. He rarely pulled them on Bond, but when he did they were always memorable.

"Let's try again, shall we?" Q said. He flipped the latch on the second crate. All four sides fell to the floor. Bond was impressed by what he saw.

"The brand new BMW 750. All the usual refinements. Machine guns, rockets—"

"Does it have a CD player?" Bond asked.

Q went on, paying no attention to him, "—GPS tracking and . . ."

He opened the car door.

". . . this is something I'm particularly proud of."

A German woman's voice, speaking in English, came from hidden speakers. "Welcome to BMW's new voice-assisted navigation system."

Bond closed the door, shutting off the recording.

"We assumed you'd pay more attention to a female voice," Q said.

"She sounded familiar. I think we've met," Bond said.

"I'm not interested in *those* escapades, Double-O Seven."

The aspen-silver-coloured car was gorgeous. Bond was pleased.

"Now, give me your gun," the major ordered.

"You can't shoot me yet," Bond protested. "I haven't broken anything."

"We're giving you this instead."

The armourer opened a box of polished wood. Inside was a new Walther P99 handgun sitting in black velvet. It was the new 9mm Parabellum, touted by Carl Walther GMBH as the gun "designed for the next century."

"I think you'll like this, Double-O Seven," Q said. He picked up the gun.

"What does it do?" Bond asked.

Q looked exasperated. He pointed to parts of the gun. "You pull this, it's called the 'trigger,' and things called 'bullets' fly out the hole in the end!"

Bond shook his head in mock disbelief. "How do you come up with these things?"

"It's a hammerless pistol with single and double action, developed in strict conformity with the technical list of requirements of the German police."

He let Bond hold it. Bond tested the weight in each hand, gripped it, looked down the sight . . .

"It uses a high-quality polymer for the frame and other parts. The magazine has a capacity of sixteen rounds, with an additional round in the chamber."

Bond liked it. It was a state-of-the-art handgun.

"Now *this* is very different," Q said, handing Bond a unique cell phone. "Kindly remember—"

" 'This is not a toy,' " Bond replied by rote.

Q demonstrated. "Talk here, listen here."

"So that's what I've been doing wrong!"

It was an Ericsson model in black. "It's got several features you may find useful: infrared fingerprint scanner, a 20,000-volt security system, detachable antenna video camera, and stun gun. It's also a remote control for your new car."

Q pressed a button on the cell phone and it opened like a book.

"We've tried to make it user-friendly, but I admit it requires a great deal of practice." He poked the tiny touch screen. "Tap twice—"

Behind them, the BMW started up. It revved the engine a couple of times, then sat there idling, awaiting a command.

With extreme caution, Q slid his finger across the touch screen. "Now, very carefully, drag your finger along this pad to steer." He did that, and the BMW went into reverse and slowly moved backward. Q pushed his finger the opposite direction. The gears changed and the car moved forward in a series of lurches. The major lifted his finger and the BMW stopped. He handed Bond the device.

"It's surprisingly difficult to drive from outside the car, but with practice . . ."

"Let's see how she responds to my touch," Bond said.

There was a squeal of tires. The BMW sped backward, did a reverse circle around a crate, spun into a boot-legger's turn, then rocketed forward toward Bond and Q. It stopped abruptly, with the bumper inches from their knees.

Bond switched off the engine and savoured the moment. Q's face was white.

"As you say, Q. With practice I might get the hang of it."

Q murmured to the heavens, "Grow up, Double-O Seven . . ."

Searchlights swung back and forth in front of the Carver Media Group Network complex. A long line of cars and limousines snaked toward a group of red-coated valets in the crescent outside the handsome brick-front building now lit spectacularly for the party. It was the kind of event that attracted the elite, the rich, and the famous. Media professionals, diplomats, businessmen and deal-seekers, artists, and even rock stars had come from all over the world. CMGN was opening its new headquarters in Hamburg.

Bond pulled up the BMW beside a valet, who opened the door for him.

Bond got out and said in German, "Don't let her push you around."

Mystified, the valet got into the car and prepared to drive it to the garage.

The car's female voice commanded, "*Seatbelten, bitte!*"

Inside the building, the party was in full swing. Bond, dressed in a black Brioni tuxedo and looking his best, gave his invitation to a woman checking passes at the door.

"Welcome, Mr. Bond. Allow me . . ." She led him into the atrium, dramatically decorated with banners for the party. The one on the left side featured the *Tomorrow* logo, and the right banner displayed the CMGN logo. Elliot Carver's face, however, was the most prominent thing on both of them. In fact, everywhere he glanced, Bond saw Elliot Carver's image on some kind of display.

The room connected two older buildings with a series of metal bridges. It was very chic. Bond thought it was just the kind of architectural design that slightly suggested self-indulgence. Elliot Carver enjoyed his wealth and liked to flaunt it.

Bond was led to a tall man who was obviously the woman's superior. He was dressed in the distinctive beige jacket that all of the public relations people seemed to be wearing. The man was talking with a striking Chinese woman in an elegant, long, silver dress. Her brown eyes met Bond's before the public relations woman could hand the man Bond's invitation. She was stunningly beautiful.

"Oh, welcome to Hamburg, Mr. Bond," the man said after looking at the invitation. "I'm Jack Trenton, VP of PR around here." The handshake was firm and hard. Bond sized him up as being some kind of bodyguard as well as a public relations officer.

Trenton continued, "And I bet you two already know each other, since you're each other's competition."

"No, I haven't had the pleasure," Bond said. He looked at her and smiled with his eyes. "My name is Bond. James Bond."

They shook hands and she said, "My name is Lin. Wai Lin. I'm with the Bank of Hong Kong. And you're . . . ?"

"With the Bank of England," he replied. It was a fairly safe cover. Coincidentally, he had recently taken a keen personal interest in finance. He would be able to fake his way through any conversation concerning money.

Bond took note of the woman. Though small in stature, she carried herself with authority and confidence. She looked to be in her late twenties or early thirties. Bond thought she was way too exotic and attractive to be a banker. He sensed something dangerous about her. He was curious and intrigued.

Wai Lin studied Bond and also came to the immediate conclusion that the Brit was not what he said he was. There was a cold streak of menace in his blue eyes. He had neatly cut black hair with a little grey on the sides. A short comma of hair hung recklessly over his right eyebrow. There was a faint scar on the right cheek, and he had a cruel, yet desirable, mouth. He was too handsome, too cool, and too sure of himself to ever have such a mundane job as banker. James Bond was some kind of detective, she thought.

Trenton said, "Let me take you up to Mr. Carver; he's looking forward to meeting you." He started to lead them through the mingling guests up the stairs toward the atrium mezzanine. As they went deeper into the bowels of the building, Bond noticed more and more distinctive red jackets worn by some tough-looking characters who were meant to be "security guards." Bond knew that they were, in fact, bodyguards—or worse.

"Isn't this great? Before it was all separate, the front office building behind us, the newspaper plant on the left, and the satellite network on the right. Now with this atrium we have the whole complex under one roof."

"Even if the one roof is a tent," Bond said.

Trenton said, good-naturedly, "Ah, but it's an award-winning tent!"

They reached the mezzanine and found Elliot Carver surrounded by guests. He was dressed in a Kenzo black, high-collared tunic that suggested a Mandarin design, and was playing the consummate host— charming, sophisticated, and distinguished. Bond found it difficult to believe that this man might be responsible for the murder of the British sailors.

"Mr. Carver," Trenton politely interrupted, "this is Mr. Bond and Miss Lin."

Carver turned to them and smiled warmly. "Ah, the new bankers!" The man turned to his guests and quipped, "I own hundreds of them." The group chuckled awkwardly.

"Did you come together?" he asked, turning back to Bond, shaking his hand.

Bond replied, "Sadly, no. We met downstairs." He noted that Carver had a firm but clammy handshake.

"Tell me, Mr. Bond. How *is* the market reacting to the crisis?"

"Currencies are off, but your stock is soaring," Bond said.

They were joined by a gracious and beautiful American woman in her early thirties. She had dark brown hair cut to her shoulders, bewitching brown eyes, and a full mouth. Her figure was smashing. She brought elegance to her flashy low-cut black dress, just as Wai Lin brought flash to her elegant one. Her magnificent cleavage was accented by a sparkling diamond necklace. Jack Trenton smiled and bowed out of the group to resume his duties.

"Ah, darling," Carver said to the woman. "Come and meet our new friends. This is Wai Lin of the Bank of Hong Kong . . ." Wai Lin shook hands with the woman. Carver turned to Bond, but before he could introduce him to his wife there was the sound of a loud slap.

Everyone in the immediate vicinity was silenced by the noise and turned to look at the group. Paris Carver stared at Bond with venom in her eyes. Bond, slightly embarrassed, lightly touched his left cheek.

"You've met my wife before, Mr. Bond?" Carver asked, perplexed. He looked from Bond to Paris for an explanation.

"Don't worry, darling," Paris said. "James and I were ancient history when I met you." She turned to Wai Lin and said, "Sorry I slapped him without asking you first, but if you've known James for more than ten minutes you will understand."

"Actually, I've known him for *less* than ten minutes," Wai Lin said, now even more fascinated by the Englishman.

"Then I have stories to tell you, honey." Mrs. Carver turned to the men and said, "We're going to powder our noses." She took Wai Lin by the arm and led her away into the crowd.

Carver scrutinized Bond and said, "My wife has quite a temper."

"And quite a right hand," he replied.

"I was very sorry to hear about Winton Beaven's illness."

"He's much better," Bond lied. "He asked me to tell you to not worry about the rumours."

"Rumours?"

"Just the usual City gossip. Meaningless. Pay no attention."

"I'm curious."

"Well, there's a silly story," Bond began, nonchalantly. "The reason you spent millions moving from London to Hamburg and from Hong Kong to Saigon was not for efficiency, but because you hate the Chinese for taking Hong Kong back and the British for letting them."

"Ridiculous."

"Then they say your satellite system is losing so much money that you're getting out of the news business. That you'll be getting into satellite navigation."

"Navigation?" Carver felt a rush of adrenaline. What was this man talking about?

"Nonsense, I know," Bond said. "There's no money in that. Is there?"

"I wouldn't know," Carver said. "Any other rumours, Mr. Bond?"

"This one's really the most absurd . . . That the real reason you moved out of London is that you wanted to be made a baron, but that they wouldn't even make you 'Sir Elliot.' "

Carver stared at Bond. He felt his jaw muscles start to hurt. Who the hell did this man think he was?

"I see you're one of them."

"Them?"

"One of those English public school salary men who think their pathetic little country will still matter as long as they look down their noses at people not as wellborn as they."

"Not at all," Bond said. "I was kicked out of Eton. I'd be happy to call you 'Lord Carver' if it would make you feel better. Tell me, Elliot. I was just wondering about your satellites. The way you've positioned yourself globally."

Carver was growing weary of this conversation. "They're merely tools for information, Mr. Bond."

"Or disinformation? Say, if you wanted to manipulate the course of governments, or people—or even a ship?" Bond said this with a perfectly straight face.

"Interesting, Mr. Bond," Carver said though clenched teeth. He was absolutely livid and was struggling to control himself in front of the guests. "You have a vivid imagination for a banker. Perhaps I should hire you to write a novel."

"I'm afraid I'd be lost at sea," Bond replied.

Carver's eyes narrowed. What did this man know?

Jack Trenton appeared at their side, obviously sensing some tension between the two men. He put on his biggest smile. "Well, sorry to pull you away, Mr. Carver. We have to get you upstairs."

Trenton started to lead Carver away from Bond, but the newslord kept his eyes locked on the man who had dared to insult him. Trenton called to Paris Carver, who was just returning with Wai Lin, "There you are, Mrs. Carver! Let me grab you and Mr. Carver . . ."

As Carver moved with Trenton and his wife, he said to Bond, "Remember what Mark Twain said, Mr. Bond: 'Never pick a fight with a man who buys ink by the barrel.'"

Aware that something was wrong between Bond and her husband, Paris Carver looked nervously at them both, then allowed herself to be led away. Bond found himself standing next to Wai Lin again.

"I hope you left something for our bank," she said.

"Plenty to go around. You have a nice chat in the ladies' room?"

"Fascinating, Mr. Bond," Wai Lin said.

"Yes?"

"Oh, I wouldn't dream of telling."

"You speak English well. Your accent . . . northern China?"

"Shanghai."

"What other languages do you know?" he asked.

"Many, Mr. Bond, French, German, Russian, Italian, Japanese, and a few different Chinese dialects. Even Danish."

"Danish?" Bond asked. "I speak Danish!"

"Do you?"

"We'll have to have a smorgasbord sometime."

At that point, the lights lowered and a spotlight hit the highest central bridge in the atrium. Elliot Carver and his wife stood there and waved to the crowd. Everyone in the building applauded and cheered. They were unaware of the private conversation the couple was having out of the sides of their mouths.

"That fellow Bond," Carver said, "was he a banker when you met him?"

"Yes." Paris hesitated a fraction of a second, just long enough to give Carver doubts.

"You're a terrible liar, my dear. And why did you slap him?"

"Just something I owed him."

"Well, now I owe him."

Jack Trenton gestured for Carver to step up to the microphone that had been set up on the bridge. Paris stepped back and Carver was left alone in the spotlight.

Shrugging off the unpleasantness that had just occurred, Carver resumed his air of self-confidence and authority. His voice was amplified throughout the atrium. Bond had to admit that the man had a mesmerizing voice that commanded attention.

"You might have heard the phrase, 'The bridge to the twenty-first century.' Well, it's not just an American political slogan, it's real: I'm standing on it! On my right, the presses are rolling twenty-four hours a day, printing the world's first global newspaper. On my left we are about to dedicate the latest broadcast center of the world's first truly global satellite network. I invite you to take a look at the ultimate expression of eighteenth-century technology, before following me across this bridge, into the twenty-first century!"

The crowd applauded. Then a line of party guests snaked out of the atrium onto a balcony overlooking the press room. Down below was a row of five-storey tall

76

newspaper printing presses. Bond and Wai Lin inched their way into the group and looked at the vast room.

"Bankers see such interesting places," she said sarcastically.

"How's banking in Hong Kong these days?"

"Under Chinese rule? Better than ever!" she said proudly.

They followed the guests back into the top level of the atrium. They were now on the platform that Carver had called the "bridge to the twenty-first century."

"Have you been on the Carver account long?" Wai Lin asked, gently probing.

"No, I flew out today. My predecessor had a gallstone attack."

"Interesting. I flew out yesterday. *My* predecessor had a kidney stone attack."

"Well, it's going around," Bond said.

They looked at each other, now more certain than ever that each of them knew that the other was hiding something.

They followed the crowd into the glass-enclosed CMGN newsroom lobby. Waiters were giving away glasses of champagne while public relations personnel urged the guests past a large model of a satellite and through double doors. Bond took two glasses from a waiter and handed one to Wai Lin.

Clinking her glass, he said, "To banking, Miss Lin."

"To banking, Mr. Bond."

They followed the herd into the CMGN newsroom, the showpiece of the party. The high-tech circular room was still bisected by the big red ribbon that had been present the night before when Carver and Gupta surreptitiously viewed the footage of the *Devonshire* massacre. Television cameras were set up around Elliot Carver, who stood in the centre of the room. A makeup girl touched him up, as he was about to be broadcast all over the world. Paris lurked at the side of the room. She watched as Carver saw Bond and Wai Lin come in. He beckoned to Stamper, the German, to come over to him. Paris didn't like Stamper. He gave her the creeps.

Carver whispered something to Stamper, and the German's eyes focused on Bond. He nodded discreetly and moved away. This did not go unnoticed by Paris.

A voice from the booth spoke through an impeccable sound system. "Ladies and gentlemen, quiet please. Thirty seconds to air."

Paris kept her eye on Stamper. He spoke into his earpiece walkie-talkie. A well-dressed security guard standing next to her suddenly put his hand to his ear. She heard him say, "Yes, Mr. Stamper. I see him. Black tux . . . Bond, got it . . . Yes, sir, it'll be taken care of."

Paris started to move away, nodding to other guests and making her way toward her old "acquaintance." There was a murmur in the room as Carver's image suddenly appeared on all the monitors.

"Ten seconds," said the voice from the booth. "Very quiet please. Five, four, three, two, one . . ."

Bond turned to speak to Wai Lin, but she was no longer at his side. He looked around quickly and noticed her slipping out of the double doors.

"Good evening," the media mogul said on camera. "I'm Elliot Carver. Tonight we celebrate the opening of our new, state-of-the-art broadcast facility for the Western Hemisphere. Joining us are our guests here in Hamburg—"

A shot of the party appeared on one of the screens. Bond noticed that he could see himself in the picture.

"—and simultaneously our friends at the Eastern Hemisphere headquarters in Saigon and our regional centers in Los Angeles, Nairobi, Buenos Aires, Tel Aviv, Moscow, and New Delhi . . ."

As Carver mentioned the cities, shots from those parties were displayed on various monitors.

Paris Carver slid up to James Bond and whispered, "What the hell did you say to upset my husband? Get out of here right now."

"But it's such a nice party," he said.

"I'm serious. You don't understand. He's going to have you beaten up or something. God knows what. He has some very strange people around him. You see that handsome German boy standing in the corner there? He's some kind of freak."

Bond had spotted Stamper earlier in the evening. The man exuded menace and an aura that suggested mental instability.

"Your husband could be involved in a terrible crime," Bond whispered back. "If he has me beaten up, well, it proves the suspicion is true."

"What kind of crime are you—damn! You should have gone!"

A guard was approaching them.

Carver, meanwhile, adroitly kept his speech on target while watching Bond and his wife. "We have been riveted by the unfolding conflict. The British claim that a pair of Chinese MiGs sank the HMS *Devonshire* in the

South China Sea, and we applaud the British for sending their fleet for proof of the sinking. How could they do otherwise, and still have self-respect? At the same time, the Chinese claim that two of their MiGs were shot down by the *Devonshire*, so we also cheer China's defiant warnings that they will not tolerate a British fleet so close to their shores . . ."

The guard said, "Excuse me, Mr. Bond. Telephone call."

Paris spoke first. "I'm sure Mr. Bond doesn't want to be disturbed right now."

"I'm sorry, ma'am. They said it was urgent."

Paris clutched Bond's forearm. "Don't go. It sounds like bad news."

"I bet it is," he said. "But then, bad news always catches up with you." He squeezed her hand to reassure her, then followed the guard toward the door.

Carver continued, "This is a terrible tragedy, of course, but also a great story, and I am proud to report that our coverage of the crisis has beaten the competition in reporting every single major development. The world is indeed watching, and they are watching CMGN!"

There was more applause. Carver relished it, especially after seeing the guard take Bond out of the room. "Now, we have to admit, it's meant a huge financial windfall for us. We are already five years ahead of our most optimistic projections. But we don't do it for the money. No. We do it for the power. The power to do good, the power to inform and educate and to make a contribution to the world. We remain dedicated to our goal—to bring the world 'Tomorrow's News, Today!'"

The room broke out into applause once again.

Outside the newsroom, Bond followed the guard back across the bridge toward the press room.

"No phones back there?" he asked, innocently.

The guard pulled a gun, a Browning 9mm semiautomatic. "We thought you'd be more comfortable over here in the office."

SIX

Party Pooper

The guard shoved Bond into an office marked "Press Manager," just off the press room balcony. 007 had just been able to glimpse a second guard in the office holding a camcorder, videotaping him, when a third guard swung a club like a baseball bat and caught Bond across the stomach. It took him completely by surprise, and he folded over in agony. The first guard, behind Bond, kicked him onto the floor. To add insult to injury, a fourth guard hiding in the corner stepped up and kicked him in the ribs.

The fourth guard said, "Mr. Carver doesn't think you're really a banker. And this guy thinks he can make you talk using only a billy club."

The second guard, the one with the video camera, moved closer to point the camera straight down at Bond. Wham! The billy club cracked viciously down on Bond's stomach again.

"Ouch," the guard said. "He might be right—I might never get to use the pliers." All of the guards laughed.

The pain was unbearable, but Bond willed himself to take stock of the situation. He noted that the room was small, containing a sofa, a glass desk, a couple of chairs, and some file cabinets. Four men. One pistol drawn. One billy club. In two seconds, he had a plan of action.

"Now, *are* you a banker?" the guard asked.

Bond still felt fire across his abdomen. Straining, he managed to say, "No. I'm an astronaut."

The fourth guard lashed out with his foot again, but this time Bond was ready. He moved with the speed of a snake striking its prey. He grabbed the guard's foot and trapped it against his side. He then whipped his own foot up and slammed it into the second guard's camcorder. The man screamed, dropped the camera, and clutched the eye that the eyepiece had been driven into. Bond snagged the video camera in midair, then hurled it into the face of the first armed guard, who dropped his gun and fell, unconscious.

Now Bond was an open target for the third guard, the one with the club. The man didn't wait. The club came smashing down at Bond's face, but 007 agilely rolled to his left and brought the fourth guard, whose leg Bond still had trapped, into the path of the club. The weapon slammed into the man, knocking him out and on top of Bond.

With his three colleagues all incapacitated, the third guard dropped the club and went for his gun. Bond pushed the unconscious guard off of him to reveal that he was pointing the Walther P99 at the third guard's face. The man froze.

"Don't you think Mr. Carver would be upset if

gunshots ruined his party? But then you'd be dead anyway, so I suppose you wouldn't care."

The guard stayed frozen.

"I guess that means you *do* care. Then toss the gun gently to that sofa."

The guard did as he was told. Bond switched the pistol to his left hand and held out his right.

"Do you have any idea what it feels like to be hit in the stomach with a billy club? Help me up."

The guard reached out and Bond grabbed the arm, raised his legs, and yanked the man down onto the soles of his shoes. He then boosted the guard up and over. The goon flipped high in the air and landed on his back on top of the glass desk, which practically exploded under him. Bond slowly got to his feet. His stomach was in terrible pain but he tried not to show it. The guard lay groaning in the ruin of the glass desk.

"It feels a bit like that," Bond said. "Party pooper."

He stepped to the door, past the first guard, who was recovering consciousness. The man struggled to bring up his gun, but Bond kicked him in the face. The gun flew across the room. The man rebounded, rolled over, and got to his knees. Bond lashed out with another kick, but this time the guard blocked it and shoved Bond hard against the door. This gave the thug time to stand up. He came at Bond with both fists, connecting once, twice . . . but Bond brought his knee up heavily into the man's abdomen. When the guard bent over, Bond pulled him up and delivered a punch that sent him hurtling across the floor and into the glass shards of the broken desk. He was out again. 007 then bent over— carefully—and took the gun. He pocketed it, then removed the earphone jack out of the walkie-talkie at the guard's hip. The chatter could then be heard aloud. It sounded routine; the guards hadn't alerted anyone else.

Bond stood and pulled the door open. Wai Lin, who had been just outside attempting to tamper with the swipe card lock, fell into the room.

"So how's your end of the banking business?" Bond asked.

Wai Lin's eyes widened when she saw the bodies strewn about the room.

"Less interesting than yours," she said.

"Security to press manager's office," came a voice from the walkie-talkie.

Bond yanked Wai Lin all the way into the room and shut the door. It locked behind her.

"Look what you've done," he said.

"What *I've* done?"

Bond led her across the room to a connecting door, pausing just long enough to pick a box of cigars out of the debris of the broken glass desk. In the adjoining room, Bond lit a cigar with his lighter.

"That's a good idea," Wai Lin said. "You have a smoke while I figure out how we get out of here."

"I think we should mingle with the crowd as they leave."

"They won't be leaving for hours."

"Maybe. Maybe not."

Bond held the cigar up under a smoke detector and waited.

Meanwhile, in the CMGN newsroom, Elliot Carver was joined in front of the cameras by a striking woman whose qualifications as a television anchor were created by a plastic surgeon in Beverly Hills.

"Now to do the honours," Carver said, "our top anchor for Europe, Miss Tamara Kelly."

Tamara stepped forward with a pair of large scissors in her hand. Miss Kelly was a tall and attractive brunette with bright, white teeth and sparkling green eyes. She smiled and waved to the crowd, and the room grew silent. It was a dramatic moment. Carver looked on with anticipation as she placed the scissors on the wide red ribbon and cut it. Simultaneously, the fire alarm went off and clouds of white powder sprayed down from the ceiling.

Everyone in the room gasped or screamed. All of the screens in the newsroom blanked out and the message "Please Stand By" appeared a moment later. Carver looked around furiously as the alarm bell was replaced by a mechanical prerecorded voice: "The automated fire alarm system has been activated. Please proceed to the nearest exit marked with a red sign. You may notice some fire retardant powder. Do not be alarmed, it is harmless to people, pets, and electronic equipment." The voice then repeated the same message in German.

Carver looked at the chaos around him with rage. The fire retardant material was swirling over his guests as they obediently began trooping toward the doors. He caught a glimpse of his wife across the room. Paris tried to suppress a smile.

Bond and Wai Lin heard the roar of people outside the office door.

"Let's go," he said.

As the herd of people clogged the mezzanine and the stairway down, James Bond and Wai Lin merged with the crowd. The powder was still sprinkling down and the voice recording repeated its message over and over.

Bond noticed several security guards looking around on all levels of the atrium. The German fellow, Stamper, was giving them instructions. Bond didn't think they could pick him out of the crowd, but it was possible. He took the lapels of his jacket and pulled them over his head, pretending to keep the powder from getting in his hair.

They passed by a guard who was scanning faces. When he looked closely at Bond, Wai Lin said, "My husband is allergic to that awful powder. You should tell Mr. Carver to change it."

The guard nodded and kept looking at faces as people streamed by. Bond and Wai Lin made it out the door and onto the pavement.

Outside the complex, the public relations staff had their hands full. They attempted to explain that the party was not over and that what happened was a false alarm, but most of the guests were unhappy that their trendy clothes had been streaked with white powder. They were all lining up for their cars. The party was a disaster.

Elliot Carver made his way outside, moving from guest to guest and imploring them to stay. Stamper caught up with him and said, "There's no sign of him, sir. We're continuing to look everywhere."

Carver nodded. He was too angry to speak. He rubbed his sore jaw, then he saw his wife talking to a group of guests. He stalked over to her and abruptly pulled her behind a pillar. He gripped her elbow hard, hurting her.

"Are you sure Mr. Bond is a banker?" he spat.

"Yes!" she said. "I told you. Stop it!"

Carver released her. Paris looked at him coldly, rubbing her arm.

"Why don't I believe you?" he asked.

"Believe what you want. It's what you always do."

He almost slapped her, but managed to control himself in front of the crowd.

"What has happened to you, Elliot?" she asked. "How can you surround yourself with people like Stamper and all these thugs?"

Carver took a deep breath. "Because they're very, very loyal. And I prize loyalty above everything. You'd better remember that."

He turned away to continue the search for Bond. Paris Carver stared after him, wondering how her husband could have changed so drastically in such a short time. He seemed to enjoy hurting her now. The elbow pinch was nothing compared to what he could do, and had done. Bond had mentioned that he was up to something criminal. She would have liked to believe that her husband couldn't possibly be involved in any illegal activities—but her instincts told her that something was definitely wrong. The evidence was all around her: those horrible men he hired as bodyguards, that goon Stamper. What was going on? Well, no matter what, Elliot Carver was not going to hurt her again.

That was the turning point. In that brief instant, Paris Carver made up her mind about something she had been considering for a long time.

Wai Lin stuck with Bond until they were outside, then deftly ducked into the crowd to lose him. She moved quickly through the guests and hoped that the British "banker" wouldn't follow her. She went around the corner of the building and stopped. She peered back from her cover and saw Bond looking about, perplexed. He probably wasn't used to someone giving him the slip so easily. Then again, Wai Lin had been first in her stealth training class.

She walked quickly away from the CMGN building, crossed the street, and stepped into the stairwell of a parking garage. She ran up the steps two at a time until she got to the third level. She unlocked a red Ferrari F550 Maranello coupe and hopped inside.

Wai Lin flipped a switch on the dashboard over the glove compartment. A panel slid open, revealing a computer monitor and fax machine. A keyboard slid out and she booted up the computer. She found the appropriate search program, then punched in the name "James Bond" and filled in "United Kingdom" for his nationality. For the field titled "Distinguishing Features," she grinned and typed "handsome."

While the message "Searching" appeared on the screen, she filed a report to her superiors. She knew she would have to sneak into the CMGN headquarters later, after everyone had left. The low-emission radar device had to be hidden somewhere in the building, and the more she thought about Carver, the more she suspected he had something to do with it. The man oozed false charm, and if there was anything she couldn't stand, it was a phony.

The search ended with no matches. Wai Lin frowned. If the man Bond was an agent for his government, then his cover was pretty good. She would try again later when she had more information. Somehow she felt that she would run into the man again.

Wai Lin shut down the computer and closed the compartment. She started the car and headed out of the parking garage. She drove past the front of the CMGN building, now cluttered with two fire trucks, a police car, and dozens of onlooking guests.

She didn't see James Bond anywhere in the crowd.

The Kempinski Hotel Atlantic in Hamburg was one of the rare landmarks in its neighborhood to escape the destruction which World War II brought to the city. One of the best luxury hotels in all of Europe, the Kempinski is located near the Aussenalster in a scenic position surrounded by trees and elegant villas. It was designed with a turn-of-the-century maritime theme that was quaint and stylish at the same time. Bond particularly liked the hotel because of its Atlantic Restaurant, which he considered to feature the finest dining in all of northern Germany. He knew ten of the fifty-five chefs personally and they always made sure that he was treated well.

Food was one of the last things on his mind, however, as he poured ice cubes into a bath towel, then wrapped it up to create a makeshift ice pack. He was standing in the bathroom of his hotel suite, examining the colourful bruise the billy club had left on his stomach. His shirt, tie, and jacket lay crumpled on the floor.

He dabbed the cold, wet towel against his belly and winced. It hurt like hell but he was pretty sure none of his internal organs had been damaged. The muscles were very sore, though. No sit-ups for a few days . . .

He and Wai Lin had slipped away from the CMGN complex easily enough. However, once they had made it to the street without being seen, Bond lost her. She vanished without a word, almost as if she had planned it that way. Bond thought she probably had. But he didn't think that he had seen the last of Wai Lin.

Bond was ready to order something from room service, eat, and go to bed. It had been a long day, and he knew that the pain in his stomach would be worse in the morning. As he came out of the bathroom holding the ice pack to his navel, he heard something scratching at the front door. He quickly dropped the pack, grabbed the Walther P99 from the holster hanging on the back of the chair, then turned out the lights. In the darkness, he crept into the darkened living room and concealed himself in an alcove by the door. He listened and waited. The latch clicked, then the door opened. Bond heard a clattering sound as someone entered the suite. He stepped forward and stuck the barrel of the Walther into the intruder's back.

Paris Carver said, "Do you always treat room service this way, James?"

Bond flicked on the lights. She was standing there with a cart laden with champagne. She was still dressed for the party.

"Thanks for the tip," she said.

Bond pocketed the gun and closed the door.

Then she noticed the horrible bruise on his belly. "James!"

Bond touched the cheek where she slapped him. "Not as bad as this one. I always wondered how I'd feel if I ever saw you again. Now I know. Was it something I said?"

"How about the words, 'I'll be right back'?" she said with tongue in cheek.

He shrugged. "Something came up."

"Something *always* came up." Paris pouted, then said, "I owed you that slap, from the days when I indulged your every sexual whim."

"You had quite a few whims of your own."

"Did I? Now that I'm married it's hard to remember." She moved into the room, making herself at home. Bond closed the door and locked it.

"You know," she said, settling on the couch. "I did love him. Once. He used to be tough and ambitious in a good way. But over the years he's become a monster. Are you too injured to open the champagne?"

"I'll manage. What are we celebrating?"

"My freedom. I left him," she said. "He's been violent before, but to strangers. I could make myself believe they deserved it. But he went too far tonight."

"It might be dangerous to leave him." The cork popped out of the champagne and he poured two glasses.

"Very. But I took only the clothes I'm wearing and my old passport. My sister in New York is leaving a prepaid ticket at the airport."

Bond handed her a glass and they tapped them together.

"To your freedom, then," he said.

After she took a large sip, she said, "So, tonight, you're a banker," she said. "Tell me, James. Do you still sleep with a gun under your pillow?"

"There is one small benefit to that."

"Really."

"Yes. I can attach a silencer to the gun."

Paris smirked. She took another sip and asked, "Now, what are you doing here? What is Elliot doing? You mentioned a crime. I take it this isn't a social visit."

"Your husband might be in trouble."

She shrugged as if to say, *What else was new?*

"The Emperor of the Air?" she replied. "If you think you're going after him, you're the one who's in trouble."

"Perhaps . . . But it's either him or someone in his organization."

Then it dawned on her what he was doing. "I see . . . And you figured you could charm the dirt out of me."

"No. That wasn't my plan."

She knew he was lying but didn't care. "Well, Mr. Banker . . ." She leaned forward and kissed him. It was hesitant at first, but then she opened her mouth and kissed him deeply. She whispered, "I hope you've come up with some more sexual whims in the last eight years. Because I plan to indulge them all."

Bond pulled her closer and kissed her again. Looking into her brown eyes, he said, "I expect I can come up with something."

He reached behind her back and unzipped her dress. Her shoulders were bare, so he kissed them lightly. She moaned softly, then pulled him tightly against her. She had needed this for a long time.

As they made love through the night, all of the images and memories of her escapades with Bond came back to Paris and she wondered why she had ever let it end. She had forgotten what it was like to be made love to by a man who cared, by a man who knew how to touch a woman, by a man who was, quite simply, a real man.

Over at the CMGN complex, the flurry of activity had died down. The fire department had checked things out and declared the supposed fire a false alarm. The guests had all left. Much of the food and champagne had gone untouched and the place was covered with the white fire retardant. The banners with Elliot Carver's face and the company logos on them were still in place, but a corner of one had come undone and it now drooped pitifully on one of the bridges in the atrium.

Up in the dark newsroom, Elliot Carver sat at a console, feeling grim. On the monitor was a tape from the camera that had covered the audience at the party. He was step-framing through a shot of Paris and the man called James Bond. She appeared to be confiding in him. Just what *was* their history?

Carver caught himself clenching his teeth. He angrily opened a drawer in the desk and pulled out a bottle of ibuprofen. He popped three tablets into his mouth and swallowed them without water.

Stamper was speaking German into the phone across the room. They were the only two people in the massive newsroom. Stamper hung up and walked over to Carver.

"I found out some things," he announced.

"Yes?"

"Mr. Bond is attached to the British Foreign Office."

"A spy, in other words," Carver said. "Go on."

"You're not going to like it."

"My wife is gone."

Stamper was surprised that he knew. Then again, the boss was always one step ahead of him. It was why he was the boss.

"She lied to me. Betrayed me. For him." He nodded toward the monitor and focused on the darkly handsome man in the frame with his wife. "Get our people out, have them bribe every skycap and hotel clerk in this city."

"Don't worry, sir. We'll find her."

"We're looking for Bond. When we find him, we'll find her."

"And then would you like me to—"

"This is my wife we're talking about," Carver said sternly. He thought a moment. Then: "Get the doctor."

SEVEN

Stop the Presses

She knew that dawn would eventually come, but when it did she wasn't ready for it. Paris Carver loved the feel of the sheets on her naked skin. She rolled over to snuggle against the man who had brought her so much pleasure for those few hours during the night, only to find that his side of the bed was empty.

She suddenly recalled the last time she had seen him. It was actually in Paris, seven years ago. She was Paris McKenna then, one of the bright new stars on the fashion scene. Paris was the daughter of a wealthy New England stockbroker, so traveling to France after graduating from Bryn Mawr was not an obstacle. She had no interest in her major in education; she had only gone to college to please her parents. Modeling was all she had really wanted to do.

She had met James Bond at a cocktail party. He was with another woman, which should have served as some kind of warning. Nevertheless, they struck up a conversation and she had been totally enchanted by him. Apparently he was attracted to her as well, for he phoned her the next evening. They had a stormy affair that lasted two months. When the romance was at its height, Paris believed that they might even get married. She had been madly in love, but one morning he left without an explanation. Perhaps it was the unwanted publicity of having their picture snapped by paparazzi at fashion shows. He didn't like his face in the papers. Paris thought she would never forgive him, but now, after last night, it seemed she had.

Four years later she met Elliot Carver. That fateful meeting also took place at a cocktail party. Carver was something of a celebrity, one of the wealthiest men on the planet, and was handsome in his way. He courted her and she succumbed to his charm. They were married three months later. She never stepped on a fashion runway again.

Bond was across the room getting dressed. Paris slipped out of bed and moved up behind him. She placed her arms gently around his stomach.

"I thought you'd be too sore to get up."

"After all that? Of course I'm sore."

"I meant where they hit you."

"Oh, no. That's fine." He turned, smiled, and kissed her lightly on the cheek.

He pulled on his shoulder holster and checked the clip in his gun. He stored some extra clips in his jacket pocket.

"I don't know many bankers who carry guns," she said.

"It's a dangerous business these days; one can't be too careful."

"Oh, James, why am I attracted to men like you? You're obviously a lot like my husband: ruthless, distant . . . there's an air of mystery about you . . ."

"You mean *mystique*, not mystery, don't you?"

"Come on, you know what I mean." She sighed. "At least you also have a kind and gentle side that surfaces every now and then. Where are you going?"

"To have a look around your husband's complex. A newspaper is very busy at dawn—this is the best time."

"You can't just go blundering around there; it's crawling with security."

Bond pretended to consider her words, then shook his head. "Still, it has to be done."

"You're trying to make me feel guilty and say something that could get you killed."

"Not really. I have to go anyway."

"You remember the lobby just outside the newsroom? With the big satellite?"

"Yes."

"There were offices back there, but they walled it up. There's some kind of lab or something there. I think. But I don't know how they get in. I remember that the offices were directly beneath the plant maintenance level of the atrium. There was a structural stairway connecting the two."

Bond kissed her. She dropped the sheet, exposing her naked body. She wrapped her arms around him and held him close.

"You sure I can't convince you to stay?" she whispered.

Bond kneaded her shoulder blades and the small of her back. He kissed her neck slowly, lingering over every inch. Paris closed her eyes and moaned softly. They clung to each other for a full minute.

Finally he said, "I'll be back soon." With that, he turned and walked out of the room.

After he had left, she said softly, "That's what you said the last time."

The day had begun much like any other business day, except that security seemed to be everywhere. The regular CMGN employees reported to their new head-quarters, ready for another routine stint of reporting the news. The printing presses were rolling, the monitors were busy, and the satellites were transmitting. The only thing different from other days was that the guards were everywhere. There was some speculation among em-ployees that last evening's false alarm had been some kind of hostile act directed at Elliot Carver.

Guards were stationed on all the levels. They made routine checks on their respective floors every ten minutes. They did, however, neglect to consider the roof as a possible means of unauthorized entry. As guards patrolled from the print room onto one of the bridges across the atrium, they were completely unaware of the figure moving over the skylight. One guard paused to light a cigarette. Above him, James Bond carefully slipped around the side of the large glass dome in the roof, unseen.

Getting up there had been easier than Bond had originally thought it would be. Since much of the building was still under construction, a workman's lift was attached to one side of the complex. At the early hour, he was able casually to don a hard hat and assume the role of a construction foreman inspecting the works.

He simply stepped onto the lift and took it up as high as it would go. From there, all he had to do was climb over a balcony and up a short ladder to the top of the building.

Another ladder led from the skylight down to the plant and maintenance area under the roof. Bond moved down into it, then crossed to a covered hatch. The controls to the hatch were under a separate locked cover. He pulled the cell phone out of his pocket and extended the antenna. At the end of the antenna was a device that served as a lockpick. It took him only seven seconds to open the cover and reveal the controls to the hatch. He pressed a green button and the hatch swung open. A stairway led down into the building. Paris Carver had a good memory.

Bond followed the stairs down into what appeared to be the laboratory that Paris had mentioned. There were drafting tables, computer tables—all empty at this hour—and, in the center, a duplicate Carver satellite. Another door led to a private office.

Bond made a quick scan of the room and then studied the satellite. It must have been a test model, something that was used for experimentation. He was about to take a look inside its circuit panel when he heard footsteps approaching. He ducked quickly down behind the satellite just as the door to the private office opened.

Henry Gupta came out, followed by the three bodyguards who had been with him in Afghanistan. Bond peered through a gap in the solar panels of the satellite and watched as Gupta paused a mere few feet away.

"We're finished with this; ship it out to the launch site," Gupta told his men. "How come there's never any food in here? Come on, I'm going to get some breakfast." Grumbling, he went out of the large steel door in the back of the lab with his thugs in tow.

Bond stepped out from behind the satellite and moved to the door of the private office. It was secured with an electronic swipe card lock. Bond produced the cell phone once again and unsnapped the bottom to reveal its stun gun terminals. He flipped the stun gun on and touched the electric arc to the lock. There was a loud *snap*. The indicator on the lock flashed green momentarily, then burned out. Bond tried the door but it didn't give. He leaned in to it and shoved—and the door clicked open.

Gupta's private office was empty and spotless, although the refuse bin was overflowing with soft drink cans and empty potato chip bags. A computer sat on a desk, and there were a few filing cabinets in the room. Bond was trained to sweep a room very quickly. He opened a drawer and saw boxes of disks and programs. In another drawer were dozens of satellite reference materials. He found thick technical books, many concerned with global positioning, radar, and composite resin technology. Bond rifled through them and saw nothing of interest. He closed the drawers and noticed mounted on the wall a large steel-framed photograph of a Carver satellite in space. His keen eye perceived that one side of the frame was slightly thicker than the other. Bond slid his fingers along the edge and found a hidden catch. He opened it and the frame swung open.

The formidable wall safe behind the frame was locked with a thumbprint scanner. Bond figured that only Gupta's fingerprints would open the safe so he needed a copy of Gupta's thumbprint.

He activated the laser built into the front of the cell phone and used it to scan the window on the safe where one's thumb was usually placed. An image of Gupta's thumb print appeared in the data screen on the cell phone. Q had envisioned this particular feature being used to call the Records Department at MI6 and get a match on any fingerprints the device scanned from a surface. Bond considered it an indication of an ingeniously designed tool when the user could improvise and find a completely different application for the device other than the one for which it was intended.

He rotated the phone and placed it so that the screen was up against the thumbprint window. Bond pushed the button on the phone marked "Safe Scan," the electric eye inside the window read the scanned thumbprint, and the safe automatically clicked open. Bond put away the phone and looked inside.

The red box that Gupta had purchased in Afghanistan was sitting in the safe. Bond took it out and opened it. Jackpot. The missing ACSES device was inside. He snapped the box shut and put it in one of his deep pockets, then closed the safe.

Bond left the private office and went back into the lab. So far, so good. He moved to the large steel doors that led to the rest of the complex. He put his ear against them and listened. It seemed quiet enough. He opened the door cautiously.

Wai Lin was stooped just outside, dressed in black from head to toe. She had been attempting to break in. The alarms started howling.

"Look what you've done!" she exclaimed.

"What *I've* done?" Bond said.

She vanished back into the stairwell, avoiding the guards who began pouring into the corridor. Bond barely had time to shut the steel doors and throw the bolt. The sound of lead slugs hitting the door was deafening.

Paris Carver finished washing her hair and wrapped it in a towel. She slipped on one of the terry-cloth robes provided by the hotel. Now she was sorry she had slapped Bond in front of her husband at the party. That single act had probably aroused Elliot's suspicions more than ever and set him off on the violent path he was on. She would make it up to James when he returned.

She had moved into the living room, ready to settle down and look at the newspaper, when there came a light tap at the door. She smiled.

Paris opened it, saying, "Well, that didn't take—"

Her heart leaped into her throat. Elliot Carver was standing outside the door with Stamper beside him. She immediately tried to slam the door in their faces, but Stamper's fingers got in the way. She shoved the door into them, but the man never seemed to feel any pain. With an enormous amount of strength, he pushed the door open and knocked her to the floor. Paris dived for the telephone, but the German grabbed her before she could get it. Carver walked in and calmly shut the door. Stamper held her easily with one hand and examined his injured fingers curiously. He licked the beads of blood off of his knuckles like a kid licking wayward drops of chocolate sauce.

Carver stepped up to Paris and held her chin in his hand.

"Elliot, please," she said, terrified. "You don't understand . . . It's not what you think . . ."

"Isn't it? Then suppose you tell me just what it is."

"You frightened me last night. I came here just to get away."

"What was it I told you last night? The one thing that I value more than anything?"

Paris swallowed hard.

"Loyalty, darling," he said. "Loyalty."

Bond ran for the stairs as the steel doors crashed open behind him. The guards swarmed into the room, shooting. 007 paused long enough to kick over the satellite, blocking the guards' path. He dashed up the stairs, came out onto the roof, and slammed the hatch cover on the pursuing men. He ran to the roof ladder but saw an armed guard at the top, waiting for him. The bullets flew, forcing Bond back against an emergency fire door leading into the media complex. Having no other choice, Bond kicked the door open and went through.

He found himself in the hallway leading to the atrium. He moved quickly into it, running across the top-level bridge. Wai Lin was at the other end, her back against the wall. She was obviously trying not to be seen by someone. The look in her eyes told him that he was in danger. He leaped out of the way just as bullets ricocheted off the metal grill he was standing on. Guards on the atrium floor were shooting up at him.

While their attention was on Bond, Wai Lin pulled a wire out of a band on her wrist and attached it to the railing. She confidently leaped over the rail, unspooling the wire as she went. Bond watched in amazement as she gave him a little wave. She descended slowly to the floor behind the guards, who were still shooting at him. Then she was gone.

Bond made a mental note to suggest a device like that to Q.

He rolled and leaped to his feet, then sprinted across the bridge. The bullets followed him as he burst through the door into the giant press room. The presses were rolling, creating a huge cacophony that gave Bond an advantage. He ran across the balcony with several guards chasing him, turned a corner, and ran straight into a wall of more guards. Without a second thought, Bond leaped over the rail of the balcony and landed on top of a huge overhead crane.

It was a machine that had two parallel arms mounted on tracks in the ceiling. Bond leaped from the first arm to the second as the nearest guard followed him from the balcony onto the first arm.

The noise of the presses was deafening, so the guards' shouts went unnoticed by the workers down below. Directly beneath the cranes was one of the printing presses. An expanse of taut blank paper was moving across it.

The guard jumped over to the second arm and confronted Bond. He swung, but Bond blocked the blow with a *Kake-te* manoeuvre. Bond's right fist shot out and connected with his opponent's chin, but the guard was strong. He surprised Bond by spinning and lashing out with his foot, successfully slamming Bond's chest with a *Ushiro-geri*. The man obviously knew a little karate of his own. Bond almost lost his balance, but he managed to gain his footing on the narrow strip of metal. It was an extremely precarious position.

The guard moved forward. Bond leaped and rammed his head into the guard's stomach. At the same time, he pulled forward on the back of the guard's knees. The man fell onto his back, but he didn't roll off the crane arm as Bond had hoped. Instead, the guard kicked Bond's left leg out from under him. Bond fell on top of the guard, who immediately wrapped his hands around Bond's throat. Bond used spear-hands to thrust up through the guard's forearms and break the hold. The guard attempted to roll his opponent off the crane, but Bond grabbed the side of the steel arm and held on tightly. Bond then viciously thrust his left elbow into the man's throat. The guard immediately released Bond and held his neck, gasping for air.

With one fluid movement, Bond pulled the guard's pistol from his holster, then pushed the man off the crane. The noise of the press drowned out the thug's scream as he fell through the taut blank paper and into the printing press. He was immediately consumed. A second later, clouds of paper streaked with red spewed all over the room.

"They'll print anything these days," Bond muttered.

He leaped off the crane onto the platform one level down from the guards. With the grace of an Olympic athlete, Bond vaulted down to the next level, and then down to the one below that.

He was now in the lower press room, which housed the huge machines. They were each loaded with three one-ton paper rolls that fed a continuous stream of paper to the presses above them. Bond ducked in-between two of the presses as guards entered that level and fanned out to search for him.

A recessed metal track about a foot wide ran along the floor, continuously moving. It was a slow but powerful conveyor that bore the one-ton paper rolls around the room. Bond stepped onto the belt and hid behind one of the large paper rolls. He prayed that the guards wouldn't notice as it moved at a funereal pace along the conveyor.

"Ink room clear," came a voice on a walkie-talkie behind him. "Check the plate room."

Just the crackle of static at the beginning of the speech had been enough for Bond. Before the broadcaster had got out the first word, Bond had spun around and fired in the direction of the walkie-talkie. A man was there, pistol raised. The slug caught the guard in the chest, but he got off a shot as he fell. The bullet ricocheted off of the roll behind Bond. He thought it was a good thing the idiot hadn't been using the earphone jack.

The shots attracted the other guards, however, and they came running toward the noise. Bond jumped off of the conveyor and launched himself toward a pair of big double doors. As the bullets flew at him, he dived through the doors.

He slid on his belly into a warehouse the size of an aeroplane hangar. Rolls of newsprint were stored in vertical stacks of five, like jumbo packages of plain toilet paper. Bond felt dwarfed by his surroundings as he rolled out of the way of the oncoming bullets. The guards followed him inside.

Several workers were driving fast Hyster 350 forklifts in the warehouse. They heard the shots and decided it was time for a coffee break. They leaped off of the forklifts and ran for the exit.

Bond took the opportunity to jump onto one of the Hysters. Its driver had just taken a large roll of paper off the top of a stack. Bond started the forklift up and drove as quickly as he could around a corner as the guards followed his lead and ran for the other abandoned Hysters.

Bond steered around a massive stack of paper rolls and got an idea. First, he spun his forklift 180 degrees. Next, he backed up to gain some runway space. Finally, he propelled the forklift forward at full speed. He rammed his own paper roll into the large tower of paper rolls, toppling them like dominoes.

On the other side of the stack, the guards on foot and on forklifts desperately attempted to run or steer out of the way of the plummeting paper rolls that crashed to the floor. The one-ton rolls shook the building, bounced, and started rolling wildly in all directions. One roll crushed a guard on foot as a steamroller would flatten concrete. A forklift was knocked over on its side. Another forklift went out of control as the guard inside tried to get out of the way. It smashed into one of the other huge paper stacks.

This stack began to topple toward Bond and the rolls fell with a resounding *boom*. He looked back and saw the bouncing rolls coming for him. He gunned the forklift, but it wasn't fast enough. Just before the rolls overtook the vehicle, Bond jumped out of the cab and caught hold of a steel structural support for the building. He clung to it as if it were a palm tree in a hurricane as the rolls of newsprint overtook the forklift and crushed it to bits. One last roll of newspaper came along at a more reasonable pace, so Bond leaped onto it and log-rolled on the top as it carried him toward the exit.

Once outside, he jumped off the paper as it rolled across the loading dock. The back end of an idling lorry was parked up against the dock. Bond discreetly slipped into it as the lorry pulled away, delivering him to safety and freedom.

Wai Lin, who was watching the building from across the street, saw Bond's escape and smiled. She had discreetly left the building during the chaos, unseen and ignored by the guards.

Her trip to Hamburg had been successful. She hadn't recovered the missing radar device, but she now knew how it was being used. Before she could point the finger at Carver and CMGN, however, she had to have further proof.

When she was safe in her own hotel room, Wai Lin contacted General Koh in Beijing and made her report. In addition to some new instructions, he gave her confidential information that was known only to the Chinese military: the British fleet was approaching China, and time was running short.

Wai Lin gathered her belongings and took a taxi to the Hamburg airport. As she boarded a plane to the Far East, she thought about James Bond once again. It was a part of Chinese nature to believe that one's destiny is predetermined, and she couldn't help feeling that hers was somehow entwined with his.

EIGHT

Death of a Friend

Stamper was positioned on the roof of the building directly across from the Kempinski Hotel Atlantic. If the Englishman was a fool, he would return to the hotel to fetch his new girlfriend. Stamper had just got off the walkie-talkie with the man he had left in charge of security back at the complex. Bond had eluded them and was now probably on his way back.

He held up the binoculars and scanned the street again. Still nothing. Maybe the spy was not as much of a gentleman as Carver perceived. Perhaps Bond was going to leave Paris to the vultures after all . . .

No, wait . . . there he was. The BMW pulled into the six-storey hotel *parkhaus*. Stamper lifted the walkie-talkie and issued a quick series of orders in German.

The BMW climbed up the ramps inside the garage and finally eased into a spot on the roof.

Inside the car, James Bond opened a concealed panel on the side of the door, revealing a combination safe. He quickly turned the dial, opened the safe, and placed the red box inside. He shut the safe, twirled the combination, and closed the secret panel.

Bond stepped out of the car with his cell phone in hand. He pressed seven buttons, eliciting seven different answering beeps from the car. He then walked calmly out of the car park, toward the hotel. Now all he needed to do was transmit a quick report to London, spend a little more time with Paris, then get out of Germany before Carver's goons found him.

Stamper watched Bond through the binoculars, then looked over at his men across the street from the car park. They were dressed in civilian clothes for this occasion, with no distinguishing red jackets. The men jumped onto a flatbed tow truck and headed toward the lot. Stamper raised his walkie-talkie and issued more orders. On cue, different groups of CMGN security guards appeared in various locations around the hotel. The building was effectively surrounded.

Bond made his way up to his suite. He heard a voice inside and wasn't able to place it. He tapped lightly on the door, but there was no answer. He drew his Walther and opened the door carefully.

The television was on in the living room, accounting for the voice he had heard. Tamara Kelly was at the CMGN anchor desk, reporting, ". . . and appeals from the Security Council have had no calming effect on London or Beijing. Now, this just in—"

"Paris?" he called.

Bond was about to click off the television when Tamara Kelly continued, "—Police in Hamburg, Germany, have discovered the partially clad body of Paris Carver, wife of the chairman of Carver Media Group and

112

owner of this network, in a Hamburg hotel suite, apparently the victim of foul play."

His heart raced. Bond stepped into the bedroom, where a second television was also broadcasting the news. The sound echoed throughout the suite.

Paris was lying motionless on the bed. He moved closer to confirm that she was dead—strangled. He was overwhelmed with shock, grief, and anger.

He never should have underestimated Carver. Until the time they met, Bond had merely suspected him. But after their initial encounter and having seen Carver's blood boil when the subject of satellite navigation came up, Bond was absolutely certain the man was guilty of tampering with the GPS and sending the *Devonshire* to the bottom of the sea. The depravity of the man had shown its ugly face then, but nothing could have prepared Bond for the demonstration of turpitude that was now displayed in front of him.

Bond cursed himself for involving her. He had lied to her when she asked him if his intention was to seduce her to gain her husband's secrets. It was precisely what his plan had been all along. He had known Paris Carver well enough to predict that she would be attracted to him again and fall for it. He hadn't planned on her marriage being on the rocks. He didn't expect that his intervention could be a catalyst that would drive Paris Carver to leave her husband.

"I have a clear shot at your head," came a soft voice from the bathroom. "Put your gun down slowly, please." He had a German accent.

Bond did as he was told.

"Now lie down on the bed next to Mrs. Carver. Watch the news."

He did it. Grimly, he looked at the television.

Tamara Kelly was saying, "Elliot Carver, en route to the CMGN Center in Saigon, is described by a spokesman as 'inexpressibly shocked.'"

The man in the bathroom said, "My name is Dr. Kaufman. I am an outstanding pistol marksman. Take my word for it."

Bond had no choice but to believe him. Out of the corner of his eye, he could see that Dr. Kaufman was sitting on one of the bedroom chairs and holding what appeared to be a Heckler & Koch P7 K3 pistol with a silencer. He looked to be in his forties, tall and slender, with thinning dark hair and glasses. His eyes drooped, giving him an intense, sinister gaze that deepened the suspicion that Dr. Kaufman was a homicidal maniac and capable of anything. For a fleeting second, Bond thought that the man resembled his dentist in London.

Kaufman had killed Paris, and he was probably the type of psycho who'd enjoyed doing it. Bond decided then and there that Dr. Kaufman would not leave the hotel alive. As he watched the news unfolding on the television, he used the time to consider all of his options. Like a chess player, Bond considered all of the possible moves and countermoves. When the right moment came, he would act.

The CMGN security guards surrounded Bond's BMW. The flatbed tow truck was ready nearby. There was a problem, though. Whenever a guard brought his fingers close to the car, he got a sharp electric shock.

Stamper, watching from the roof, wondered what the hell was taking them so long. He panned the binoculars over to the front entrance of the hotel. Two Hamburg policemen were speaking with his two men stationed there. Damn, they got to the hotel too quickly! His men needed to break into the BMW before the policemen got up to the suite.

Stamper shouted instructions into his walkie-talkie.

One of the men by the BMW acknowledged the order. He took a hammer out of the truck, and slammed it into the BMW's side window. It didn't even chip. The man barked an order to another guard, who drew a pistol and shot at the window. The bullets bounced off, almost hitting them.

Bond watched the news in fascination. It was a complete news story listing all the details of events that were yet to happen.

"Police also discovered the body of a man believed to be the occupant of the hotel suite," Tamara said, "the victim of a self-inflicted gunshot wound. Police refused to speculate on a motive in the murder-suicide. All of us at CMGN would like to extend our deepest—"

Dr. Kaufman clicked off the television and said, "That story goes on the air in an hour. The police are on the way to the hotel as we speak."

"Tomorrow's news, today," Bond said.

Think, he willed himself. Bond glanced around the room. The good doctor was too far away for Bond to jump him. If the man was as good a shot as he claimed . . .

"She seemed quite intelligent," Dr. Kaufman said. "But she called her sister in New York. Didn't she realize her husband owns the satellite that relays overseas calls?"

"It won't look like a suicide if you shoot me from over

115

there." He needed more time to think. Maybe he could get the man to talk longer . . .

Dr. Kaufman said, patronizingly, "Mr. Bond, I am a professor of forensic medicine. Believe me, I can shoot from back here and create the proper powder burns on your hands, the scorching around the wound."

"Is this your hobby, then?"

"Certainly not," Kaufman said. He seemed offended. "I am very well paid. I go all over the world. I am especially good at the celebrity overdose. Now—"

He suddenly shouted, "Mr. Stamper! Stop yelling in my ear!"

It took Bond a second to realize Kaufman was talking to his earphone walkie-talkie.

"You're not serious?" he said into the headpiece. "Surely the auto club— All right, I'll ask." Kaufman made a facial expression that implied that the whole world was full of fools and that he was the only being with any brains.

"This is so embarrassing," he said to Bond. "It seems there is a red box they need from your car. And they can't turn off the car alarm. They want me to make you shut it off. I don't know what to say, I feel like an idiot. A car alarm!"

Perfect! Bond thought.

"To be fair, it is a bit tricky," he said.

"I'm to torture you if you don't do it."

"Do you have a doctorate in that, too?"

"No," Kaufman said. He grinned broadly. "That *is* more of a hobby. But I'm very gifted."

"I believe you. The alarm works from my cell phone. I'll just—"

He started to reach for his jacket that he had left lying on the floor.

"No, no," Kaufman said, pointing the gun. "I'll do it."

Very carefully, keeping his distance from Bond, Kaufman lifted the jacket and extracted the cell phone. He dropped the jacket and held up the phone.

"All right, what do I do?" he asked. "No tricks."

"You hit Recall, Three, Send," Bond said.

Dr. Kaufman looked at Bond and decided that it sounded harmless enough. He slowly pressed the three buttons and—*zap!*—the phone's stun gun went off in his hands. He yelped and dropped the phone as Bond catapulted off the bed. He caught Kaufman's gun hand. They slammed against the floor and rolled. Kaufman was wiry and agile, enabling him to jump to his feet first. Bond tackled him and he fell back onto the bed. Bond leaped on top of him and grabbed the gun hand again. This time, he held on tightly. Possessing the superior strength, Bond implacably forced the hand back so that the pistol was aiming at Kaufman's own head.

"Wait," Kaufman pleaded. "Don't. I'm just a professional, doing a job."

"Me too," Bond said.

The gun fired and Dr. Kaufman's head exploded into a bloody mess.

Bond stood up. Most of the time Bond didn't like killing. He had been forced to do it a number of times in the line of duty. There were quite a few instances in which he had been assigned to kill men in cold blood. Bond always performed the duty efficiently and effectively, but he never enjoyed it. Only a few times during his illustrious career had he ever felt really good about killing someone—someone who, he felt, deserved it.

117

This was such a case. It wasn't going to bring back Paris, but at least he had partially evened the score for her.

He dropped the gun, wiped the blood off his face with Kaufman's own jacket, then moved over to the bed to look at Paris again. With a heavy heart, he leaned over and kissed her lightly on the lips.

Then came the loud banging on the suite door. The two Hamburg policemen were outside, shouting in German for him to open up. By the time they broke down the door, the suite was empty except for the two dead bodies.

Bond had slipped out onto the balcony. It was a short jump from there to a lower balcony, and one more leap to the roof of the *parkhaus* behind the hotel.

Stamper, looking through the binoculars, witnessed Bond's escape. He spoke urgently into his walkie-talkie.

Bond sprinted out onto the ramp, toward the car. He stopped when he saw the guards still attempting to break into the BMW. He pulled out the cell phone and punched a button.

A thick cloud of tear gas erupted from the BMW, engulfing the guards. They gagged and choked, staggering away from the vehicle. More guards a few feet away saw Bond and drew their guns. Bond pressed another button on the cell phone and the BMW roared to life.

With its lights blazing, the car skidded out of the parking place in reverse and scattered the choking guards. Then it changed gears and shot toward Bond just as the men began to fire. Bond ducked behind the bulletproof body of the automobile.

A bullet ricocheted dangerously close to him. Bond turned to see a guard coming down the ramp behind him. He opened the closest door and dived into the backseat as the bullets pinged against the BMW.

Using the device's remote control feature, Bond was able to view the front of the car on the cell phone's little monitor. He threw the car into gear and drove it down the ramp, all the while lying low in the backseat.

The BMW forced the guards to jump out of its way as it barreled down the ramp. Bond took this opportunity to climb into the front seat as the car continued moving. He activated the dashboard GPS screen, which instantly charted the car's path through the garage. With the aid of this device, he was able to anticipate turns and obstacles before he could actually see them. The electronic map indicated that a vehicle was behind him, hot in pursuit. In a few seconds, Bond saw the black sedan in the rearview mirror. Guards on either side were leaning out of it and firing pistols at him. One of them had an MP5K 9mm submachine gun and was shooting wildly at the BMW.

Bond whipped around a ramp turn, then reached out and hit a switch on the dashboard. A small hatch opened beneath the back of the car, spilling a stream of metal tire spikes.

The sedan slid around the turn and ran over the spikes, and all four tires were punctured at once. The quadruple blowout caused the car to slam into the wall. Its windshield shattered into a spiderweb from the impact of the guards' heads.

Bond felt exhiliration behind the wheel of the car. Its 5.4-litre, 322 horsepower SOHC V-12 engine allowed the BMW to accelerate from zero to sixty-two miles per hour in 6.6 seconds. Aside from Q's special modifications, the car came equipped with sixteen-inch, multispoke-designed alloy wheels, halogen headlights, leather seats, and dual air bags.

The BMW kept going down to the next level as

another sedan raced toward Bond from around the turn ahead. Bond flicked another dashboard switch.

A rocket fired out of the front of the car, blowing the sedan off the path and into the air. It bounced against the ceiling and landed upside down on a row of parked cars.

Bond made it to the ground floor and raced toward the exit. Suddenly, the steel shutters lowered, sealing off the exit.

Bond increased his speed, and flicked the switch on the dashboard again. Another rocket fired and hit the steel shutters. It only dented them.

He slammed on the brakes and turned the wheel, skidding 180 degrees and just bouncing the rear of the car off the shutters. That had been too close. He had no choice now but to race back up the garage.

The guards were assembling behind the steel spikes that Bond had left earlier. Now they had him, they thought. They readied their guns as they heard the BMW approaching.

The car zoomed onto their level with great speed, and Bond drove right over the spikes. The tires blew out, but the car kept moving as they reinflated. Another one of Q's extras had saved his life. The guards looked on with incredulity, then opened fire behind him.

The car moved up the ramp, forcing the guards out of the way.

Stamper shouted into his walkie-talkie when he heard what was happening in the garage. One man on the fourth level acknowledged the order and opened a large steel case. He pulled out a handheld rocket launcher, loaded it with a shell, and positioned himself just beyond the ramp up to the fifth level. He aimed the rocket launcher at the far end of the floor, ready to pull the trigger as soon as he saw Bond's car. Sure enough, the BMW came barreling up the ramp and turned toward him. The guard took one last aim and fired the shell.

Bond saw the man at the other end of the level as he flew up the ramp. The GPS device on the dashboard flashed, and the electronic German voice said, "Rocket attack. Please turn right."

Using nothing more than reflex, Bond spun the wheel to the right. The rocket flew by the car and demolished a parked Jaguar as Bond's car disappeared up the ramp in front of the shooter.

The guards piled into two more sedans and raced after him.

As soon as the car made it to the fifth level, which was devoid of guards, Bond slowed down and opened the door. He turned the knob on the combination safe, opened it, and snatched the red box. Then he jumped, rolled, and took some cover between two parked vehicles. He operated the remote control and kept the car moving up the ramp. The two sedans passed him in pursuit. The men didn't notice that he was no longer inside the car.

Bond pushed a button on the remote, releasing magnetic flash grenades from the rear of the BMW. The first sedan exploded spectacularly, and the second one plowed into its rear with a resounding screech.

The BMW made it back to the roof and went straight for the railing. Bond increased the speed, then watched the monitor on his cell phone go blank.

The car forcefully broke through the railing and flew off the roof of the high garage. It sailed out into the air, then plummeted six storeys and crashed into the front window of an Avis Rent-a-Car office.

The street was suddenly alive with activity—pedestrians screamed and ran, cars stopped in the street, and sirens were heard in the distance.

Up on the car park roof, the guards jumped from their cars and raced to the gap in the railing. They stared down at the wrecked BMW. Where was its driver? What the hell had happened?

Bond folded the cell phone, put it in his pocket next to the red box, then discreetly slipped down the stairs of the *parkhaus*. He emerged on the street as police arrived and onlookers were beginning to crowd around. A woman wearing an Avis jacket was among them.

Bond stepped up to her and took his rental agreement from his jacket. He handed it to her and said, "I left the keys in the car."

As he walked away, the woman stared at him blankly.

From the rooftop across the street, Stamper watched through his binoculars as Bond strolled away from the scene. There was nothing he could do about it. None of his men were answering their walkie-talkies.

Hell, he hated giving a bad report to the boss.

NINE

Carver

Elliot Carver popped six hundred milligrams of ibuprofen into his mouth and swallowed the tablets with a swig of gin. The problem with air travel was that he liked to yawn and chew gum to combat ear pressure— but those very acts aggravated his TMJ. He closed his eyes and rubbed his cheeks with both hands. The jaw muscles were tense and hard as nails.

Carver and his immediate entourage were flying in a private British Aerospace 125 Corporate 800B jet that he used for travel between Germany and Saigon. It was a horrendous trip, but he had done it many times. He usually had the pilot stop in Bombay for a breather. The plane was just entering India's airspace.

As he looked out of the window at the clouds floating against the bright blue sky, Carver attempted to summon up some feelings of melancholy. She was gone . . . his wife was gone. It was curious that he didn't feel more grief, no matter how hard he tried. Perhaps he had really grown tired of her after all. It hadn't been the difficult decision he had thought it would be to have Stamper do away with her.

Besides, she was a lying, betraying bitch who slept with the enemy.

Carver coldly dismissed Paris from his mind and heart. She had been wonderful when it was good, but it hadn't been good for a long time. He had married her for her looks and sexual compatibility. He would find other women to replace her. Elliot Carver could have his pick. After all, he was on his way to becoming the most powerful man in the world.

If only his father could see him now, he thought. Lord Roverman, the supreme bastard . . . May he rot in hell . . .

Many years ago, Carver had been told by a pediatric psychiatrist that he had a "complex" about his father. It was why he acted up in school and bullied younger children. He had been starved for attention. At the time, he couldn't understand what that had to do with his father. He never *saw* his father. His father pretended that his son didn't exist. Carver had to force the old man to pay attention to him, and that was much later.

Carver understood the analysis now. He could intellectualize it, now that he was an adult and had experience behind him. He could see why never knowing one's true mother, because she had died giving birth, might have an impact on one's emotional development. He completely comprehended the notion that his lust for power, fame, and money was in actuality his way of getting back at the father, who sired him and then abandoned him.

For God's sake, Carver thought, the man gave little Elliot away to a poor Chinese family. He actually paid them fifty pounds to take the useless, unwanted child. And his wife—his *late* wife—often wondered why he was always so "bitter."

Why are you always such a grouch? she would ask in that New England accent of hers.

Why are you always such a bitch? he wanted to reply. He finally did say it when he lost his temper one night. That was the first time he had struck her. She never called him a "grouch" again.

He blamed it all on his father. Why not? He was a suitable scapegoat. For the first time in a several years, Elliot Carver's thoughts drifted back to the fateful events of 1974.

He was a successful news anchor in Hong Kong. Elliot Carver had become something of a celebrity in the colony. He was considered very handsome, and he had acquired the nickname of "The Emperor of the Air." Four years shy of turning thirty, Carver had long since left the Chinese family who had brought him up and he had struck out on his own. He was living modestly in a flat in the Wanchai district of the island.

Women were never a problem, although he found that they grew tiresome after a while. He never had a steady girlfriend for any length of time, and he had no desire to get married. Girls were always available to him, though. His television good looks and celebrity status assured him of that. He made use of women, and sometimes he wasn't very nice about it. There had been a sticky situation when one of the girls in the secretarial pool at the television station accused him of sexual harassment, but this was long before the days when that kind of charge was taken seriously. The girl was persuaded to drop the accusation or find another place to work. She chose to leave Hong Kong altogether.

Carver had learned about his true parents when he was fourteen years old. His foster parents never broached the subject, but one day young Elliot asked them about it. After all, they were Chinese and he wasn't. They finally told him that his mother had died when he was born. His father, who was unable to raise Elliot himself, persuaded them to adopt him. It was a few years later when Carver found out the entire truth. At his foster father's deathbed, Elliot demanded to know everything. The old man finally told him all—that they were paid a mere fifty pounds, which at the time was a sum they needed badly, and made to promise not to reveal who Elliot's real father was.

"Who was he?" Carver wanted to know.

Lord Roverman. *The* Lord Roverman. Owner of a dozen newspapers in England. He and Lady Roverman had two grown daughters. Lord Roverman, a wealthy Conservative peer.

Further probing about his mother revealed that she was a German working as a prostitute in the same Wanchai district where Carver lived. The poor woman died in pain bringing Elliot into the world. Lord Roverman had apparently been attempting to expand his news empire to Hong Kong and was working in the colony for over a year. He had cheated on his wife, slept with a prostitute, and got her pregnant. Roverman was present at the birth, and after the woman died he made the arrangements to pay for Elliot's adoption.

Learning all of this sent Elliot Carver into an abyss of depression. He had been a troublesome child, considered "unruly" in school. Trouble with the law inevitably

126

followed, and he was forced to submit to teenage counseling. The depression stayed with Carver until he turned twenty-one. At that time he finished, to his own surprise, a college course in television broadcasting. He auditioned for a job at a station and was taken on as a weatherman. In less than a year, he was an anchor.

Elliot Carver had found the occupation that he was good at. The first few years were rewarding, but he became restless. He wasn't satisfied. He often thought about his father and the enormous wealth and business opportunities that should be his. Why shouldn't he share in the empire his father had created? What could *he,* Elliot Carver, not do with such power? He could go on and create something bigger, something more influential and important.

Obsessed with the idea of confronting his father and revealing to him the success his forgotten son had become, Carver made the trip to England in 1974. He didn't warn the old man, whom he had never spoken to, that he was coming.

Elliot knew a German fellow in Hong Kong by the name of Hans Kriegler. Kriegler, a thin and wiry weasel of a man, worked at a bar frequented by soldiers and sailors. There was a certain seediness to the bar that suggested underworld criminal activity. Elliot had been drawn to the bar for various reasons, mainly for casual female companionship, and for the occasional drink. He got to know Kriegler, whose job was "security." In fact, Kriegler was a crook. He was a thief and a smuggler— admirable skills that the man readily admitted to having— and most likely he was a murderer, too. Kriegler never admitted the latter, but he slyly implied that he was capable of the act and Carver believed him. Kriegler enjoyed the status of being the friend of a celebrity newscaster.

Before traveling to England, Elliot Carver asked Kriegler for some help. Did he know anyone in England? Was there any way Kriegler could help him "get" to his father? Did he have any ideas?

Kriegler extracted the whole story from Carver and thought about it. "Have you considered blackmail?" he asked. The German outlined a plan for Carver and gave him a name to contact.

When Carver got to England, he thought he would try the straight approach first. He went to Lord Roverman's office and presented himself. He asked to see his father, to which the secretary replied, "Lord Roverman has no son. You must be mistaken." Carver scribbled a note that read: "Your Hong Kong son Elliot Carver is here to see you." He handed it to the woman and asked her to deliver it. Ten minutes later, he was shown into Lord Roverman's private office.

His father was not what Carver had expected. He seemed frailer than his photographs suggested. He was older than Carver had thought. He walked into the room with a cane and sat down at the desk and asked, "What do you want?"

No hello. No "It's nice to see you, son." None of that.

"What do I want?" Carver asked. "I came all the way to England to meet you!"

Lord Roverman looked uncomfortable. "Now that you've met me, what do you want?"

"What makes you think I want anything?" Carver asked.

Roverman leaned forward and said, "My wife and daughters must not know of your existence, do you hear me? No one must know. It could ruin me. Now, suppose I give you a thousand pounds to go back to Hong Kong and never come back."

Carver seethed inside. "So, you think you can just throw a bit of money around to get rid of me again? I'm sorry, *Father,* but it won't be so easy this time."

Carver got up and left the room. That was the last time he saw the man alive.

Hans Kriegler had put Carver in touch with another German fellow, a scoundrel who was known only as "Mr. Schnitzler." Mr. Schnitzler was also a man of dubious employment history and purportedly made his current living fronting stolen jewels. A teenage German boy by the name of Stamper was living with Schnitzler at the time. Carver was immediately struck by Stamper's strangeness. He wasn't quite . . . normal. The kid wasn't playing with a full deck of cards; even so, the boy possessed some kind of aura that frightened Carver. There was pure menace behind his eyes, and Carver never forgot that.

Schnitzler had Stamper follow Lord Roverman for a few days. The kid came back with some interesting information. It seemed that the good newspaper baron had a wife in Mayfair and a mistress in Soho. Some snapshots were taken of Roverman entering and leaving the other woman's flat.

Carver thought this was a start, but somehow it wasn't damaging enough. He wanted something really scandalous. Could they find out more from the mistress? Was Roverman into anything . . . unusual?

Schnitzler went to work on the mistress, a lower-class barmaid and part-time prostitute whose loyalty to Lord Roverman went only so far. If enough money was thrown her way, she could be persuaded to cooperate. For six hundred pounds, she allowed Schnitzler and Stamper to set up a hidden camera in her flat. She promised that they would certainly catch the MP doing some things he wouldn't want *anyone* to know about.

When Lord Roverman came around for his weekly visit, young Stamper was waiting inside the bedroom cupboard. He had already seen some wild sexual activity in his short lifetime, but nothing quite compared to this. Lord Roverman liked to dress up in a Catholic school-girls' uniform and be spanked by his disciplining mistress. Not only were some colourful photos taken of the act, but ten minutes of 8mm footage was shot as well. Already, Stamper showed a talent for capturing odd events on film.

Schnitzler phoned Lord Roverman at his office a week later. It took some doing to get connected to the man himself, but once the newspaper baron was on the phone, the German laid it all out.

"Oh, hello, Roverman," the German said, omitting the title. "I just wanted you to know that we have in our possession some rather compromising photos of you and a young woman in Soho. Let's see, she has red hair and a much more ample bosom than your wife . . . You know the one I mean, right?"

Lord Roverman's heart began to race. All he could say was "Yes."

"Anyway, I'm sure you wouldn't want these photos to make their way to your wife, would you?"

"No."

"Well, then, we're just going to have to make sure that doesn't happen. Oh, I almost forgot—we also have a bit of film, too. About ten minutes' worth. How did you ever get a schoolgirls' uniform in your size? It must have been specially made, I imagine?"

This time the MP said nothing.

"Ah well, that's unimportant," Schnitzler said. "Look, we'll be in touch, all right?"

Schnitzler hung up the phone. Carver sat across from him with a look of anticipation.

"That will give him something to think about," Schnitzler said. "We'll let him sweat for a few days, then call him back."

"What if he calls the police?" Carver asked.

"He won't."

They waited a week. Lord Roverman went about his business, but the phone call preyed heavily on his mind. He could barely look his wife in the face, for he knew she would be devastated by the revelation of his infidelities. When the next phone call finally came, Roverman recognized the voice and asked, "What is it you want?"

"Want? What makes you think we *want* anything?" Schnitzler asked.

"You must want something, or else you would not be doing this."

"My dear man, that would be blackmail."

"That's what this is, isn't it?"

"Not at all. We just want to make sure these photos and that film don't get into the hands of the press."

"The press?" Lord Roverman was really worried now. "I thought you were threatening to show them to my wife."

"Well, sir, if the press got hold of them, your wife *would* see them, would she not?"

"You bastard," Roverman said quietly.

No demands were made this time either. Schnitzler

131

hung up and turned to Carver. He said, "Go back to Hong Kong. For this to work, we'll have to wait awhile. It's best that you are not in England anyway."

So Carver went back to Hong Kong and resumed his job as a television anchor while Schnitzler and his young aide Stamper worked Lord Roverman until the old man was ready to sign away his life. Instructions came to him in an unmarked, clean envelope. Lord Roverman was required to rewrite his will. Upon his death, sole ownership of his entire newspaper empire had to go to his illegitimate son Elliot Carver. Proof of the new will had to be sent to a specific post office box within the week.

So that was it, Roverman thought. The sin of the father had returned at last to haunt him.

Roverman did as he was told. The truth about his indiscretion in Hong Kong would come out eventually, but at least the other matter would be kept quiet. It was a small price to pay, he thought, in the long run. After all, when young Carver inherited the business, *he* would be dead! Why should it matter to him then?

Schnitzler received a copy of the will and immediately canceled the post office box. He informed Carver in Hong Kong that it was done.

"Very good. Go on to the next step," Carver ordered.

"You remember the monetary arrangements we made?" Schnitzler asked him.

"Of course. But I can't very well pay you until I have control of the business, can I?"

Schnitzler sent young Stamper to work again. For a second time they bribed the mistress, whom Roverman had stopped seeing. They wanted her to plead with the MP and ask him to come by and see her one last time. Lord Roverman was hesitant, but the woman promised him something "special." It was too big a temptation, so Roverman agreed.

Stamper was hiding in the flat when Lord Roverman arrived. The front door was mysteriously unlocked and ajar. Roverman entered the flat, calling the woman's name. There was no answer. He stepped into the bedroom and saw his mistress's strangled body on the bed.

Before he could retreat in horror, Stamper stepped up behind him and put a gun to his back.

"Turn around," the youth said.

Roverman couldn't speak. He did as he was told.

Stamper placed the gun on the bed beside the old man and said, "The boss thinks that it wouldn't be too good for your reputation to be involved with this woman's murder. You've already left your fingerprints on the front door. We have evidence that you used to see her. It could be presented to the police that she might have been blackmailing you with compromising photos and a film. If you think that it would be bad if the world found out you like to dress up in a schoolgirl's uniform, what do you think would happen if everyone thought you were a murderer?"

"What are you going to do?" Roverman asked.

"I'm leaving the gun there for your convenience," Stamper said. Even at his age, he was already a cool professional. "It has one bullet in it. I'll wait in the next room." Stamper got up to leave, then turned around and added, "Oh, and don't try to shoot me with it. That will just add one more murder to your list of crimes."

Stamper went into the sitting room, removed his gloves, and sat down with a copy of a men's magazine. Ten minutes later, he heard a loud gunshot in the bedroom.

133

Senior police officers investigating the case were personal friends of Roverman, so they withheld certain information from the press. All that was reported was that Lord Roverman had shot himself in the flat owned by a woman who had gone "missing." As the mistress turned out to be a prostitute with no family, her murder was kept confidential.

Elliot Carver was notified of his inheritance within a month. He flew to London and, expressing shock and dismay, accepted all of the legal papers and responsibility of his new fortune from Roverman's lawyers. He met his stepmother and stepsisters briefly. They were completely baffled as to why Roverman would have changed his will and given the entire business to a son he never mentioned. They contested it, but the courts eventually ruled in Carver's favour.

Elliot Carver became a wealthy newspaper baron before reaching the age of thirty. It was only a matter of time before he had built a global enterprise of media communications and create the Carver Media Group Network.

He had discovered that power, after all, was what he liked more than anything. He found that there was no better way to gain omnipotence than by manipulating the news. It was the perfect means to increase his company's earnings and his personal wealth. Disasters, riots, and political conflicts made the best headlines for Carver Newspapers and earned the top ratings on Carver Television. By heavily promoting Carver Films' new animated movie in all its media, there would not be a parent on earth who could avoid feeling guilty if they didn't see the movie, and visit Carver's toy stores and theme parks. Micro-Carver Software consistently released bug-laden products so that consumers would be forced to upgrade for years. Carver Publishing capitalized on celebrity murders and drug overdoses.

It had taken a while, but Carver had proven that the ability to *create* news and then influence the world's perception of it gave him the power of a god.

The plane began its descent into Bombay for its short layover and refueling.

Carver turned and looked at Stamper. The cretin was snoring in his seat. The lucky bastard, Carver thought. He himself never could sleep on an airplane. He envied anyone else that could, even the peanuts-for-brains goon he had hired to head up his security operations ten years after the incidents in London. Stamper had proven himself to be useful in many ways, even though he didn't have a respectable IQ. Usually, Stamper's particular talents were quite effective.

Stamper had messed things up in a big way this time, though. The spy Bond had infiltrated his offices, seduced his wife, and, worst of all, got away. Bond was just smarter, that's all. That's why he escaped. Well, he thought, Elliot Carver was even smarter. He would stay one step ahead of the agent from MI6.

"Stamper!" he shouted.

The German woke with a start. "Huh? What?"

"I know just where Bond will go next," Carver said. "I want you to meet him there."

TEN

From the Sky to the Sea

The United States Air Force SH-3 Sea King helicopter circled overhead until the pilot got clearance to land. The copter, manufactured in Britain, had been enormously successful as a rescue and executive transport vehicle. It descended slowly, finally settling on a remote landing pad situated away from the main activity of the base. A squad of USAF MPs and two civilians stood at attention, awaiting the VIP who had come on the chopper.

James Bond hadn't been to Japan in a long time, and he had visited Okinawa only once. He stepped out of the Sea King, dressed in Royal Navy uniform. He still held the rank of commander, even though he was officially in the Reserves. He returned the MPs' salutes as he held Gupta's red box in his left hand.

The sergeant shouted, "At ease!"

One of the civilians, a big man in a suit that screamed CIA, stepped forward.

"Hey, Jim! You owe me big-time, pal," he said in a broad southern American accent.

Bond shook Jack Wade's hand. They had worked together in the past, in Russia. Despite the popular notion that MI6 and the CIA never get along, Bond enjoyed working with his American counterparts. His closest friend, Felix Leiter, was once in the CIA. They had been a good team, and Bond had called on Leiter's help even after he had left the CIA to work for Pinkerton's Detective Agency. It had been a while since Bond had seen him, since Leiter was semiretired and was freelancing somewhere in Texas.

Jack Wade, another Texan, came from a different mould to Leiter. Big and burly, he was more of a "good ol' boy" who got on Bond's nerves at times. What was particularly annoying was the man's insistence on calling him "Jim." He was a good agent, though, and he had a ton of connections. Wade had once got Bond out of a difficult situation.

"You were able to bring it?" Bond asked him.

"M called me herself, at home," he said, grinning. "I was honoured to do her a favour."

He turned to the other civilian, a mild-mannered man in his forties.

"Jim, this is Dr. Dave Greenwalt. He's head of our lab that developed this whole thing." Bond thought he was the antithesis of Dr. Kaufman in Hamburg. Dr. Greenwalt couldn't hurt a flea if he tried. They shook hands.

"Okay, Dave, bring it out," Wade cheerfully commanded.

Dave looked at Wade as if the man were mad. "Out? Right outside? Here?"

138

Wade rolled his eyes. "We're in the middle of a U.S. Air Force base and we have twenty armed guards with us. I think it's okay."

The doctor nodded, then walked over to the sergeant. The sergeant barked some orders and the men began to unload a large cart from an armoured truck. Wade pulled Bond aside.

"Now, Jim, I don't mean to be disrespectful of our gallant British allies," he said, "but *what the hell are your people smoking?* Don't they realize that China has you outnumbered? By about a *billion*? And your Navy, do they think this is 1863? You got your six itty-bitty ships right next to a humongous Chinese MiG base!"

"M nearly got fired for saying the same thing," Bond said.

"Ah, that explains it." Wade grinned even wider. "Your own people think you're liars and idiots, and you have to go off on your own. Hell, that's every day at the CIA."

"Say, Jack?" Bond asked.

"Yeah, Jim?"

"You still have that tattoo on your arse?"

Wade glared at him. He wasn't particularly proud of the white rose on his right hip inscribed with name of his third wife, "Muffy."

Dr. Greenwalt called to them, "Okay, it's ready."

Sitting on the cart was a GPS device, similar to the one that was on the *Devonshire*. Next to it was a safe. Dr. Greenwalt unlocked the safe and removed an Atomic Clock Signal Encoding System device. He placed it on the cart.

"Sorry to be paranoid, but this is one of our most closely guarded secrets," Dr. Greenwalt said. "There are only twenty-two of— *Ahhhh!*"

He yelled as if he had suddenly seen a snake. Bond had taken out his own ACSES device from the red box and tossed it casually next to the one from the safe.

"My God, Jim!" Wade said.

"Meet number twenty-three," Bond said. "Our gift to the CIA. You can keep it, *if* you stop calling me Jim."

After he recovered from the shock, Dr. Greenwalt hooked both ACSES devices up to his GPS equipment. The two other men watched over his shoulder as the monitor came to life. There were two overlapping circles, but they didn't match exactly.

"Someone's tampered with this. Look."

"Could that send a ship off course?" Bond asked.

"Yes," Greenwalt said. "If you could send this signal from a satellite."

"If I tell you where the ship thought it was when it went down, can you work out where it actually went down?"

"No problem."

"There would have to be a very small margin for error. Say, from here to the edge of the runway."

That was about fifty yards. Dr. Greenwalt held up his two hands like someone showing the size of a fish.

"I can put you between here and here."

"That would be lovely," Bond said. He turned to Wade. "I, um, have one other little favour to ask."

The USAF C-130 was fighting for altitude in the thin air very close to its maximum ceiling. It had left Okinawa in

140

the morning and by midday had reached the airspace over southeast Asia.

James Bond was decked out in diving gear with fins strapped to his chest and a parachute on his back. He was also equipped with two bulky devices on each wrist—an altimeter and a GPS receiver.

An Air Force staff sergeant rechecked Bond's equipment, shaking his head, while Jack Wade looked on with a creased brow.

"My God," Wade said. "How did you talk me into this?"

The sergeant said, "Did I forget to say it's negative fifty-four degrees up here?"

"No, actually, you didn't forget," Bond said.

The pilot announced over the intercom, "Two minutes!"

"And did I mention that you have a five-mile free fall?" the sergeant asked. "And when your chute opens at two hundred feet, you hit the water like a sack of cement?"

"Yes. In fact, you've mentioned all that more than once," Bond said.

"I must be crazy," said Wade. "You're going to die and I'll spend the rest of my life testifying before Congress. Hell, there has to be a better way."

"Unfortunately not. I have to avoid the radars of both the Chinese and British fleets, and hit the water right between them. A HALO jump is the only way."

"Is that true?"

"Afraid so," the sergeant confirmed. "You fly in *above* the radar and don't pop the chute until you're *below* the radar. The High Altitude Low Opening jump was invented for that."

"See?" Bond said. He smiled at Wade.

"I mean," the sergeant continued, "who would try something that had a forty percent risk of serious injury, if it *wasn't* the only way?"

The pilot announced, "One minute."

"And you've never done this before?" Wade asked.

"First time for everything," Bond said. He adjusted his face mask and checked the regulator.

"And very few ever try it twice," the sergeant said. "Even if they don't drown or break their necks."

"I have a very bad feeling about this," Wade lamented. "You won't sue us, will you?"

Dr. Dave Greenwalt was fiddling with his GPS machine a few feet away. He piped up. "Hey, I just noticed something."

"Okay! Position's wrong! Back to base!" Wade said hopefully.

"No," Greenwalt said, pointing to the screen. "The position's right. This is where the ship thought it was, and here is where it actually is. No, it's just a weird little thing."

"Thirty seconds! Jump stations!" the pilot announced.

The staff sergeant helped Bond to the jump door as Wade began to panic. "Come on, what? What?"

"Well, see that little island?" Greenwalt pointed to the screen.

"Yeah?"

"That means that where he's jumping, between the British and Chinese fleets . . ."

"Ten seconds!" the pilot called.

The big rear door opened, revealing an amazing view of the earth. They were at such a high altitude that its

142

curvature could be seen. Wade paid no attention to the spectacular sight.

"Spit it out, damn it!"

"Well, technically it's in territorial waters, but not China. It's Vietnam."

"Vietnam!" Wade exclaimed. "He's jumping into *Vietnam*? Are there any U.S. markings on him?"

"Only on the parachute," the sergeant said. Then he thought about it. "And the tanks. Oh, and the flippers, the dry suit . . ." His words turned into a mumble as his own brow creased as heavily as Wade's.

"You can't!" Wade pleaded to Bond. "The Vietnamese are nuts! No telling what they'll do! They think Stalin is still alive! You'll be captured, tortured, reeducated, purged!"

The pilot was counting down, ". . . two . . . one . . . zero!"

Bond gave a little wave to Jack Wade and stepped out into space. Wade closed his eyes and held his head.

"I bet they send me to prison," he moaned.

The conventional way of dropping airborne troops into a target site was at a low altitude. Parachutes were automatically opened by static lines at approximately a thousand feet, and soldiers would drift down completely exposed and at the mercy of enemy fire. If the plane came in at a higher altitude, jumpers drifted too far from the intended drop zone. HALO was the answer to these problems. By flying twenty thousand feet or more above the objective, carriers avoided radar. The divers used free fall and skydiving techniques to maintain stability and guide themselves to the proper opening point. The chute was deployed at a dangerously low altitude, and the jumper would land immediately afterward.

Bond held his arms crossed over his chest as he dropped straight down through the mesosphere. The feeling was frighteningly exhilarating. He had made many jumps in his lifetime, but nothing like this. He was well aware of the dangers involved. As the staff sergeant had mentioned again and again, Bond could freeze to death before he hit the water. Or he could break his legs or neck on impact with the water. Timing was critical. The parachute had to open at just the precise moment. Otherwise, if he was too early, radar would pick him up. If he was too late, then he would fail Her Majesty's government and not be given a second chance—ever again.

He wore a DUI CF200 dry suit made of a highly durable crushed neoprene designed for extremely cold conditions. Even so, it felt as if the icy wind pierced through it as he plummeted faster and faster. Dry suits were much warmer than wet suits because one usually wore undergarments beneath the suit. Bond wore a track suit, and this provided a layer of air against his skin instead of moisture. Additionally, the insulating ability of a dry suit remained nearly constant at any depth. The suit came with hard-sole boots and neoprene gloves, as well as a neoprene hood. His other standard equipment included an integrated weight system, which eliminated the need for a weight belt by holding lead weight in the backpack; a SeaQuest Black Diamond buoyancy compensator made of 840-denier nylon; two aluminum Dacor cylinders, each containing 100 cubic feet of air compressed to 3200 psi; a Dacor Extreme Plus regulator that used a demand air system; a Mares ESA mask with lenses in front, both sides, and underneath, allowing a very wide field of vision; Mares Plana Avanti fins; and a SeaQuest/Suunto EON Lux air-integrated dive computer that sensed depth and computed how much time remained at that depth before decompression was needed and also indicated how slow an ascent must be. The one item that Bond always liked to wear when diving was his old battle-scarred Rolex Submariner. It had a built-in extender, enabling it to be worn over the latex cuff of the dry suit.

Bond kept an eye on the wrist altimeter. It was spinning toward zero like a watch zipping backward through time. He glanced at the GPS tracking device. It showed a crosshair target, with a flashing red dot jittering far from its center.

007 maneuvered in the air, forcing his body to move closer to the target. The flashing red dot slowly drifted toward the center of the crosshairs as he burst through the atmospheric cloud layer. The skyscraper-sized clouds made a *whoomph-whoomph* sound as his body cut through them.

Suddenly, the clouds opened up, giving way to a dazzling view of the blue ocean below. It was rushing toward him at a terrifying speed.

Bond's shock chute blasted open with a bang, jolting him hard. It stopped the fall for just a second or two—then he hit the ocean surface feet first. A huge geyser of water marked his entrance. There wasn't a soul or ship in sight that might have witnessed the drop.

The water didn't feel as cold as the air above the clouds. It was downright balmy by comparison. Bond immediately detached his parachute cords and continued to sink straight down. His wrist altimeter was winding well below minus one hundred feet.

Bond flipped over so that he was diving headfirst. He rolled onto his back, angling downward as he put on his fins. Righting himself, he continued his descent. He vented his buoyancy compensator with the dump valve. He held the inflator-deflator valve in his left hand throughout the descent so that he could add or release air from the BC at any time. Bond breathed slowly and equalized his ears every two feet. He controlled the rate of descent by the average amount of air he kept in his lungs, and kept a neutral buoyancy by adding short bursts of air to the BC.

He had drunk plenty of water before the jump. Dehydration is one of the leading contributing factors in the development of decompression sickness. SCUBA diving can dehydrate a person in four ways. First, the breathing air has had all or most of the moisture removed. A second reason is immersion diuresis, which causes one's bladder to fill up quickly with urine. A third reason is the potential salt intake from the ocean. Finally, wearing the suit itself can lead to dehydration.

Bond swam down, kicking from the hip. He knew to minimize sculling his arms, as that was an ineffective means of propulsion. It had been a while since he had been underwater. With the danger of the HALO jump behind him, he was actually beginning to enjoy the dive.

The water of the South China Sea was remarkably different from that of the Caribbean. It was darker hued and a bit murkier. Visibility was only about six metres. The marine life didn't seem as populous, probably due to pollution. Still, the world below the surface was an environment that never ceased to fill Bond with awe. He imagined that he would feel the same way about space-walking. Each was an alien environment that humans were not meant to traverse—yet man had conquered both.

The silence of the sea was broken only by the rhythmic bursts of bubbles escaping from his mouthpiece as he exhaled. He felt totally alone, a stranger in a strange land. Although the first rule of diving is never dive solo, Bond rarely had a buddy to accompany him on the work he usually had to do. When he went diving for recreation in the Caribbean, a Jamaican boy of seventeen named Ramsey would often accompany him. Together they would hunt for octopus or crabs. Ramsey was a terrific little cook, too; Bond had paid him well to act as his chef on several occasions.

As he swam, Bond suddenly found himself thinking about his house in Jamaica. He had named it Shamelady, after the indigenous plant that curled when it was touched. He missed the faint strains of reggae coming from over the hill, the Blue Mountain coffee, the friendliness of the people . . .

Get hold of yourself, Bond thought. Jamaica was a long way from here, and he had a job to do.

Now, where was the bloody ship? It had to be here somewhere. If his and M's suspicions weren't correct, then they might as well throw the first stone at China.

He looked at the altimeter. He was approaching the two hundred feet mark.

Bond swam a little deeper, peering through the dark water for any sign of wreckage. What looked like a mass of coral and rocks became clearer as he swam closer. It was the nose of one of the wrecked MiG-21s. Other bits and pieces of the plane were scattered about on the ocean floor. Bond examined the damage and recognized the tell-tale signs of a missile attack. The nose looked as if it had been ripped away from the fuselage and was stuck into the ground. The severed edge was black and burnt. There was no sign of the other half of the plane.

He entered the back end of the nose and made his way through jagged edges of metal to the cockpit. The pilot, bloated and white, was still strapped into his seat. His arms floated eerily at his sides as if he were trying to fly. The eyes had been plucked away by sea predators. The windscreen was smashed and the instrument panel looked completely destroyed. Fish swam in and out of the holes in the glass, using the cockpit as shelter from larger sea creatures.

Finding the MiG confirmed what he and M had suspected. The *Devonshire* had gone down exactly where the Chinese had claimed the ship had been. Something *had* misled the crew into thinking they were at a different position. If Carver was responsible, what was his motive? Why would he want to start a war between China and Britain? Were some of the stories true? Was he really that upset about the handover? Bond didn't believe it. It must be something else. From what he knew about Carver, Bond believed the man was only interested in making money and expanding his power base.

He left the cockpit and swam out the way he had come. He continued the search along the sandy ocean floor, passing two manta rays. A school of groupers swam past him toward a dark shape ahead. What looked like a huge crest of a mountain sticking up from the ocean floor transformed itself into the shape of a ship as Bond moved closer.

He had found it. HMS *Devonshire* was on her side, balanced on the edge of what looked like a bottomless crevasse.

ELEVEN

The Sunken Tomb

James Bond switched on a halogen torch with a xenon bulb and swam closer to the hulk of the sunken frigate. The starboard side was facing upwards, and the bow was angling down off the edge of the crevasse. He began at the stern and swam along the hull, examining it carefully with the torch. He moved along forward, past the mainmast and onto the forecastle area. In time, he found the hole approximately thirty metres from the bow. He carefully inspected the damage, relying on his training in the Royal Navy to ascertain that a conventional torpedo hadn't sunk the ship.

Before entering the frigate, Bond checked the dive computer. He didn't have a whole lot of time. The descent had taken three minutes, and he had already spent another five or so in the cockpit of the MiG. At best, he had about ten minutes before he would have to begin the slow, careful ascent. According to the computer, he would have to spend forty-five minutes to an hour ascending, including stops along the way.

Without wasting another moment, he swam through the hole and entered the dark undersea tomb.

Bond had investigated a number of sunken vessels during his career, but nothing had given him the creeps like this one. The enormity of the ship was intimidating and navigation through it was akin to swimming through a maze. Because the ship was on its side, all the interiors were tilted unnaturally. Tables and chairs were bolted to the side walls, cabinets on the ceiling had swung open, and heavy items littered what was now the floor. It was very disorienting. Bond had to keep reminding himself that "turning left" really meant "going down" and "turning right" meant "going up."

As he swam through, he checked doorways, dodged floating debris, and looked for any clues that might tell him what had happened.

The damage done to the *Devonshire* was definitely not caused by a torpedo. Torpedoes didn't turn corners and go up and down stairways. The corridors looked as if some gigantic sea monster had bitten its way through them. There were jagged streaks cut into the walls, running the entire length of Bond's journey. The only way he could describe it was that it looked as if something had *drilled* its way through the ship. Not only that, the drill had known where it was going.

As he swam, Bond began to feel the pressure building in his ears, a common side effect of diving. He equalized the pressure by initiating what was called the "Toynbee manoeuvre," which was a method of opening the Eustachian tubes by blocking the nostrils, closing the mouth, and swallowing. When that didn't work, the "Valsalva manoeuvre" could be used, but it had to be executed carefully. This was a method of opening the tubes by blocking the nostrils, closing the mouth, and gently trying to exhale. Experienced divers knew that the middle-ear spaces must be equalized frequently to prevent the painful "trapdoor effect" of closed Eustachian tubes held tight by the pressure.

Bond swam down a stairwell into the black. His torch cast streaks of yellow over the darkness, creating eerie shadows. It was fortunate that he knew his way around a frigate. It was quite possible to get lost or trapped in the hulk due to the disorienting angle and its area.

The only sounds he could hear were his own breathing, the hiss of the regulator, and the air bubbles flowing out of the mouthpiece. Every now and then there was a creak of metal as the ship moved slightly on the cliff edge. Bond knew he would have to be careful and not dislodge anything heavy, the redistribution of weight might cause the frigate to plunge into the crevasse completely.

He moved into the lower deck main corridor, getting closer to where he wanted to go: the munitions room. He swam across the corridor and had to push a large metal box out of the way of the smashed door. When he did so, a hand dropped in front of his face mask. Startled, Bond grabbed the wrist and lashed out at the attacker—but then realized he was fighting a dead sailor, bloated and grotesque. Bond pushed the corpse away, feeling revulsion.

Bond followed the trail of "teeth" marks into the mess, where he found more bodies. They were suspended in the water with arms and legs outstretched in that peculiar sky-diving position. Some predatory fish had got in and were feeding on the cadavers. Bond waved the torch and they scattered. Then he moved onward, out of the subterranean sepulchre.

He finally made it to the missile and munitions room, which was where the trail made by the undersea drill ended. He shone his torch over the array of cruise missiles and counted six fixed to the floor on numbered pads below conveyor tubes leading to the ship's deck. The closest pad, number seven, was empty. Bond moved closer to the pad's clamps and examined them. They bore clear marks of having been cut with a welder's torch. So! The stakes had been raised even higher. Whoever was responsible for this had a cruise missile in their possession.

Bond had accomplished what he had come to do. He had the proof that the Devonshire was indeed in territorial waters when she was sunk. And he could see from the fact that none of her small missiles were missing that the *Devonshire* had not fired at the Chinese MiGs. He raised his torch and started to swim back but he encountered the tip of a CO-2 spear gun thrust directly against his chest—with a mysterious diver was at its other end. The stranger had the gun in one hand, and a cyalume torch in the other.

Bond held out his hands to show that he was unarmed and began to back away slowly. The other diver kept the spear gun trained on him. Bond quickly ducked into a dark passageway. Acting quickly, he removed a gun from a vari-pistol box mounted on the wall. He fired a flare at the diver. It streaked past, temporarily blinding the attacker. Bond swam forward and knocked the spear gun out of the diver's hand, then yanked off the diver's face mask.

Thick black hair billowed around the diver's face—it was Wai Lin. She opened her eyes, unsheathed a knife from her belt, and swam at Bond. He caught her arm and struggled with her a moment, trying to indicate that he was a friend. Recognition set in, and she stopped. She was as surprised as he was. He helped her get her face mask back on and clear it, then he motioned upward. The sooner they got out of there, the better. She nodded. They had overstayed their computerized allotted time.

Perhaps it was their movements or the length of time the ship had been underwater, but something caused a torpedo stack to suddenly come undone. Its heavy arsenal had been straining against the supports and finally snapped them. The torpedoes fell, clanged like church bells, and slid across the tilted room. Bond and Wai Lin felt a sudden lurch as the *Devonshire* moved with the shifting weight. The ship was tilting farther into the crevasse it was precariously perched upon. Bond tried to communicate that they had to get out *now*. Wai Lin's eyes were wide; she had read his thoughts.

They bolted for the exit, but one of the torpedoes brushed against a munitions locker and sheared off its padlock. The locker burst open and heavy boxes of ammunition tumbled out and down to the end of the room. This shift in weight was just enough to cause the ship to begin a slow slide over the precipice. The walls shuddered with a huge groan as the *Devonshire* lurched and scraped over the rocks. An ammunition box slid by Wai Lin, slamming the door shut, trapping them inside. Bond and Wai Lin froze as the ship tilted even farther, howling with a horrible noise of grating metal on rock.

Bond spent a few seconds trying to move the ammunition box, but it was much too heavy. He gave up and swam to a hatch covering a ventilator shaft, possibly the only exit from the room. He tugged on it and was joined by Wai Lin. It was stuck, of course. Together, they put everything they had into it and finally dislodged it. Bond gestured for her to go first. She swam inside and he followed.

They moved through the tilted shaft as the ship settled. It wouldn't plummet any more than it had—they hoped.

They swam for thirty seconds or so, then came to a section of the shaft that was bent in one spot. Something on the other side of the shaft wall had dislodged and pushed in the metal like a mold. It bulged into their swimming space and they couldn't get past it. Bond tried to squeeze through the tight space but only managed to get himself stuck. With a superhuman effort, he pushed with his arms against the wall in an attempt to widen the shaft. Whatever had bent the wall was extremely heavy. A lifetime of morning push-ups paid off as he slowly inched the shaft wall outward. The tanks on his back served as a cushion. Finally, he bent the wall back far enough into its original shape for them to swim through.

The swimmers hurried on as they felt yet another lunge, indicating that the *Devonshire* could still drop off the cliff at any time. They soon came to a fork in the shaft. Both paths were too small for Bond and Wai Lin to pass through wearing their aqualungs.

Bond removed his tanks and shoved them into one of the tubes, then swam in afterward and pushed the tanks in front of him. Wai Lin followed suit, removing her Sherwood dual 100s and sticking them into the other tube. She was moving along when the tanks struck a pipe in the shaft. The regulator valve broke and the compressed air exploded into bubbles as it escaped. It was useless. She dropped her tanks and quickly turned back. She swam out of the tube, then went into the passage behind Bond. He was several yards ahead of her.

The ship lurched again, this time with great force. The shaft was spinning, and the ship was now rolling down the side of the cliff. Bond swam for his life, completely unaware that Wai Lin was behind him struggling to catch up before she could no longer hold her breath.

Bond made it to the end of the tube and kicked the shaft open. He wasn't sure what deck he was on, but the room was moving. There was no time to lose. He grabbed his regulator and sucked in some air. Wai Lin weakly emerged from the tube and he saw that she was without tanks. He grabbed her and pressed the mask into her mouth. He held her tightly as she filled her lungs. He took another moment to replace the tanks on his back.

This time the ship made a tremendous noise as it finally toppled off of the cliff and began to spiral downward into the seemingly bottomless deep. Bond grabbed Wai Lin and swam upward, dodging walls and debris, navigating through the maze by instinct. He finally saw the hatch to the upper deck and shot for it.

As the spinning frigate of doom continued to descend, the two tiny figures emerged from its deck and started swimming slowly toward the surface. They held each other, breathing alternately through the same regulator. It was a good thing Bond had brought along a pony bottle, which was a small extra cylinder of air mounted on a bracket between the two larger tanks. The additional air would come in handy, since they were both now using the same oxygen. Careful not to ascend too quickly, they enjoyed clinging to each other and sharing the same air. The panic of certain death eventually subsided and they relaxed. They stopped briefly at forty feet, then again at thirty feet. They spent more time, nearly thirty minutes, at twenty feet. This was required to prevent an attack of the bends later.

Finally, they broke the surface together and treaded water. The sun was beating down.

Bond casually said, "It's the opportunities for travel that I like best about banking."

She smiled and said, "Well, let's not forget the expense account. And the company junk."

She nodded toward a Chinese junk floating nearby. It was coming to pick her up. The junk was a typical Chinese boat with bluff lines, a high poop and overhanging stem, no keel, high pole masts, and a deep rudder. A Chinese man came forward and waved to her. Bond realized that it was a good thing he had run into Wai Lin. Jack Wade had made provisions for him to be picked up by a Vietnamese fisherman working for the CIA, but the boat was nowhere to be seen. Perhaps Wade's admonitions were not out of line after all.

The junk moved closer, bobbing in the water. The Chinese man gathered a line and started to throw it to Wai Lin and her companion. He called to her in Chinese— then, without warning, the man's chest exploded with a spurt of blood and flesh. A harpoon had struck him from behind and was now sticking out of him at a grotesque angle. The man's look of surprise turned to a blank stare as his body crumbled and fell off the boat.

Behind him was Stamper, holding the spear gun.

It was the middle of the night in London.

Bill Tanner was monitoring the British fleet on a special screen in his office at MI6 headquarters. Six ships were in position in the South China Sea. The Chinese fleet had assembled off the coast of Vietnam, waiting for the other side to make the first move. They had sent a message that if the British fleet had not withdrawn by midnight of the next day, then *they* would make the first move. It was already the next day in Vietnam. At the moment, the situation was a stalemate.

There was still no word from 007. After receiving his report from Hamburg, M had ordered Bond to fly to Okinawa and meet up with the CIA. His instructions were to find the *Devonshire*. M's only hope of solving the crisis was to convince the men in the situation room that the frigate had been sent off course and sunk where the Chinese claimed it had been. Surely by now Bond would have made it to the site.

The phone buzzed.

"Tanner here," he said into it.

"Any word?" It was M. She was at home, probably unable to sleep.

"Not yet."

"I'm coming in."

"It's the middle of the night, ma'am. Surely you need your sleep."

"I managed to get a couple of hours," she said wearily.

"I'll come and relieve you. You need some rest, too."

"I'm fine, you don't have to—"

"I *want* to come in," she said. "I'll be there in an hour."

Tanner replaced the phone and sighed. Emergency situations always tended to motivate people to go the extra distance. Like Bond, he had gone from unfounded misgivings about their new boss to an undeniable respect for her. Since this whole thing started, she had stuck to her guns and stood up to the men who were her superiors in the situation room. The minister of defence was a sensible man, but there were others—particularly Admiral Roebuck—who were downright foolish. Tanner sometimes wondered how men like him got to be in the positions they were in. If Sir Miles Messervy had still been in the big chair at MI6, Roebuck wouldn't have a leg to stand on.

The phone buzzed again.

"Tanner here."

"This is Wade, CIA," came a welcome, boisterous voice.

"Yes, Mr. Wade," Tanner said. "This is a secure line. Go ahead."

"Is M there?"

"She's on her way. I'm her chief of staff."

"Oh, hell, it's the damned middle of the night there, ain't it . . . I lose all track of time these days. Sorry about that."

"It's all right. I'm awake, obviously. Did 007 get off all right?"

"Yeah, yeah. I ought to have my head examined for letting him do that. Yeah, we dropped him over Vietnamese territory. We were able to pinpoint where the *Devonshire* thought she was, and where we think she actually went down. Your hunch just may be right. According to our top expert on GPS and satellite navigation, you *are* right. But you know, my Vietnamese man who was going to pick him up couldn't find him afterwards."

"Don't worry about that," Tanner said. "007 is the most resourceful man I know. He wouldn't have gone in without a backup plan."

"If you say so. Anyway, we haven't heard a word from him. We can't fly in to look for him, either. All U.S.

personnel have received orders to stay out of the area because your ships are just begging to be fired at by the Chinese."

"I understand. You've done what you can do. Thank you."

"Look—do me a favour, will you?" Wade asked.

"Sure."

"When you hear from him, give me a ring. I want to know he's okay."

"Will do."

"He's really a pain in the ass at times, but he's a damned good field agent."

"We know. Thanks again."

"Besides, he owes me now. I'll have to hit him up for a night in swinging London."

"I think you'll find that London doesn't swing much anymore, Mr. Wade, but I'm sure we can find some entertainment for you."

"Sounds great, Chief."

"The name's Tanner."

"Thanks, Tanner."

"My pleasure. Thank *you*."

Tanner hung up, then stood and walked over to the window. He looked out over the Thames, at the twinkling lights of nighttime London. He thought about his friend and hoped that he was indeed all right. He had known James Bond for many years. Amid the numerous changes and reorganisations that MI6 had gone through, he and Bond had remained among the few veterans. They had seen administrations come and go. Tanner wondered what he would do if anything ever happened to Bond. He didn't think he would have much reason to continue his job. He had been given the option of retiring when Sir

Miles Messervy left the service, but he had elected to remain with the new M. He was glad he had.

Without Bond at MI6, though, Tanner would seriously consider getting out. An MI6 without 007 would be a boat without a paddle. Of course, if he left, there was the problem of having somewhere to go—if war broke out with China, what would happen to Britain? Would there still be a country in which he could build the cottage he'd always wanted and retire? Would the war reach all the way to the Western Hemisphere? If it did, other nations were likely to get involved. He dreaded the thought that Great Britain might be one of the instigators of World War Three. It certainly wouldn't be pretty.

Come on, James, Tanner thought. Do your magic. Give it the old 007 touch. I know you can do it. You've got to.

They were allowed to put on dry clothes, then Bond and Wai Lin were handcuffed together. Her own clothes had been aboard the ship—black trousers, a white T-shirt, a red Prada jacket, and tennis shoes. Bond had to make do with a dead sailor's blue linen shirt, black trousers, and tennis shoes that were a bit too small.

"We're going to take a little ride," Stamper told them.

"Where are we going?" Bond asked.

"Mr. Carver wants a word with you. We're going to the Saigon headquarters."

"We're going all the way to Saigon in this boat?"

"Shut up and sit down, both of you," Stamper ordered. He pointed the spear gun at Bond. As the couple sat on the floor of the boat, the German said, "A helicopter will pick us up."

The man turned and joined two other men armed with

automatics. Apparently they had killed all of the Chinese crew and dumped the bodies overboard. The three men spoke in German and laughed.

Bond and Wai Lin looked at each other. Somehow they were able to read each other's thoughts: Should we make a move now? There's only three of them. No, let's wait and see what Carver is up to . . .

Without saying a word, they both relaxed and inexplicably felt completely comfortable with the fact that their lot had been thrown in with the person they were handcuffed to. They were each confident that the other one was totally reliable and had no problem with taking risks.

"Shipwrecks make the best spots for diving, don't they?" she whispered after a moment.

"Notice anything unusual about this one?" he asked.

"Apart from the missing missile and the torpedo holes in the side?"

"Interesting torpedo that drills in, goes around corners, and does not explode."

Her brow creased as she realized he was right.

"Stop the talking," Stamper said.

The boat sailed on as the minutes ticked away. Soon it would be noon. The Chinese deadline for the British fleet to withdraw was only twelve hours away.

TWELVE

The Streets of Saigon

When South Vietnam fell to the Communist government of Hanoi in 1975, the city of Saigon was renamed Ho Chi Minh City. However, the inhabitants of the city never quite got accustomed to the new name and still preferred Saigon. Since it could not be abolished completely, the authorities conceded to a compromise and kept the name Saigon for the center of Ho Chi Minh City. Therefore, today the entire city is officially called Ho Chi Minh City, while the center is still known as Saigon.

According to one theory, the name Saigon was used officially for the first time around 1698, when Lord Nguyen Phuc Chu sent Nguyen Huu Canh to the southern region of Vietnam to create districts and establish a government. The strategic location provided opportunities for trade, commerce, and military importance. Saigon began to grow; by 1772 the many canals were filled to form streets. In the mid nineteenth century, the French and Spanish invaded the port city, an event which was the precursor to a series of long struggles between the people of Vietnam and the French. France was ultimately defeated in 1954, but the country was divided into North and South Vietnam. Saigon became the center of resettlement for many people from the north. After three tumultuous decades, Saigon/Ho Chi Minh City remains the country's cultural center. It is bustling with business and commerce, and is often called the "Pearl of the Orient" by the press. Saigon boasts a population of over five million people and is one of the densest urban areas in the world. It is not uncommon to find houses with ground floors converted into a business front while several families share living quarters on the upper levels.

Elliot Carver moved his Asian headquarters from Hong Kong to Vietnam shortly before the transition. He had expanded considerably and was in need of more space. He moved the entire operation to a fifty-storey building in the center of Ho Chi Minh City, an area that had recently developed into an expensive tourist trap. The CMGN headquarters was still under construction, and bamboo scaffolding and green construction netting were clearly visible on two sides of it. A large vinyl banner featuring Elliot Carver's huge face was draped on one side of the building.

Bond and Wai Lin had been brought to the CMGN Building by an Augusta A 109 helicopter designed for civilian use. The corporation was one of the few high-profile companies that had moved into Vietnam since the days of the war, and the government appreciated it. The Vietnamese were pleased to have the prestigious network on their soil, and so far they had done nothing to try to influence the news.

The copter landed on the roof and the couple were led, still handcuffed together, in front of Stamper and his thugs, into an elevator. The two guards had obtained Mach-10 submachine guns in the helicopter and were now pointing them at Bond and Wai Lin's spines.

As they walked down the hall, a Chinese man in an unmarked uniform followed by two bodyguards passed them. Wai Lin felt a rush of adrenaline and blinked twice when she saw him. It was General Chang! So he *was* hiding out in Saigon! Too bad there was nothing she could do about it at the moment. General Chang paid no attention to the handcuffed couple and marched straight down the hall into another room.

Bond and Wai Lin turned a corner and passed something a little more bizarre. A young Chinese man who looked as if he were a Michael Jackson impersonator walked by them, followed by an entourage of transsexual-looking Asians. Bond thought they were a completely incongruous sight, considering the situation he and Wai Lin were in. Wai Lin, on the other hand, frowned when she saw them. After the shock of seeing General Chang, she wasn't at all surprised to see none other than the Crown Prince Hung and his band of merry men. They disappeared down the hall behind the General.

Outside Carver's office, Stamper told the guards in German, "Hold them here and wait." Then he opened the office door and went inside alone.

"You seemed to recognize those two," Bond said quietly.

"Yes," she whispered. "Very bad credit risks."

Stamper opened the door and ushered them into what was essentially a smaller version of the newsroom in Hamburg. It was a private news studio, all in an office of opulent luxury. A large conference table was covered with a map of southeast Asia and small models showing the Chinese and British fleet positions. Elliot Carver was on the other side of the office, looking at monitors. Henry Gupta sat in front of the desk, working on a PC.

Stamper stepped over to Carver and whispered in his ear.

"Really?" Carver said. "You do? We'll see."

Stamper moved away and looked at the floor as Carver turned to Bond and Wai Lin.

"Well, Mr. Bond," he said. "Only yesterday my wife died in your bed. And you came halfway around the world to die in my office. How fitting. Had I known who you were, I would have taken care of you differently."

Wai Lin glanced at Bond. She knew the handsome Englishman was something special, but she didn't know what Carver knew.

Carver noticed Wai Lin's glance and said, "Is it possible you have not been introduced? James Bond, Double-O Seven, of the British Secret Service. Wai Lin, of the People's External Security Force. Have you seen the papers? Your two countries are about to go to war."

"Of course we know each other," Bond said. "We've been working together. We know your entire plan. We've reported to our chiefs. You won't be writing tomorrow's headlines. You'll be in them."

Carver feigned chest pains and mocked him. "Oh my God! They know all! We're doomed! We have to

168

surrender!" Carver raised his hands. Stamper, not grasping the sarcasm, hesitantly raised his hands, too.

Gupta snorted. "Don't be a moron," he said to Stamper. "The boss is kidding."

Stamper, embarrassed, glared at Gupta.

"Now, now, Stamper is quite brilliant in his own way," Carver said, placating his top henchman. He looked at Bond and Wai Lin and said, "You might find this interesting."

He picked up a sharp silver letter opener and handed it to Stamper.

"Stab yourself in the leg," Carver ordered him, casually.

Stamper took the instrument and shoved it deep into the meat of his thigh without effort or hesitation.

"Like this?" he asked, as if he had brushed away a fly.

"You see?" Carver said. "Stamper is very unusual— his pain and pleasure centers are reversed. That's helped to make him a perfect killing machine."

He asked Stamper, "Would you rather take that out, or leave it in your leg?"

"Could I leave it in?" Stamper asked, completely serious. "For a while?"

"This is a special treat for Stamper," Carver said, "as we couldn't have him stabbing himself seven times a day."

"He'd go blind," Bond quipped.

"Very funny. But not so funny for Miss Lin. He doesn't often have sexual desires, but when he does— well, I have some of the most incredible videotapes."

"Better be careful, then," said Bond. "*You'll* go blind."

Carver ignored him. "Normally the next step would be

to have Stamper torture you both for information. But I honestly don't care what you know. So he's going to torture you both for fun. And don't think it will be better for Miss Lin because he finds her attractive."

"No," Bond said. "That would make it worse."

"Not really. Because as much as he loves pain for himself, he loves it ten times more on other people."

"We know you stole a nuclear warhead cruise missile from the *Devonshire* after forcing the ship off course," Bond said.

"Really?" Gupta asked. "How?"

"Don't look at me, Mr. Bond," Carver said. "I couldn't care less if you satisfy my friend's curiosity or not." Carver sat down in a swivel chair in front of the monitors.

"You used your satellite to send the ship into Chinese waters, using a stolen ACSES device—"

Wai Lin picked up the narrative. "—and you shot down the two Chinese MiGs that came to investigate, to spark a crisis between our two countries."

"Then at midnight tonight," Bond continued, "when the Chinese have threatened to move against our fleet, you'll fire the missile at Beijing, knowing they will retaliate against London."

Wai Lin built upon this information. "And you'll have the traitor, General Chang, install that Swiss playboy who calls himself Crown Prince Hung, the heir of the Ming Dynasty, as the new Emperor of China."

"Only none of this will work," Bond said, "because your whole plan is known."

Gupta was a little shaken by this. Carver noticed and said, "Don't worry."

He rubbed his chin in thought, then turned the chair to Bond and Wai Lin and said, "Very good. Only two minor things wrong. First, it *will* all work, even if you have reported it, which of course you haven't because you've both just figured it out now. That was my little mistake, of course, letting you see General Chang and the next Emperor in the hall. But you were each diving in the wreck alone. Which means that, whatever you've reported, your governments don't believe you. That's the point, isn't it? The truth is not relevant. What matters is what the media reports."

"And the second minor thing?" Bond asked.

"If you really understood anything, you'd know why I won't wait for midnight. I plan to start the war an hour after dusk, to catch the maximum potential viewership in the Western Hemisphere time zones. If you think the Gulf War was great for my ratings, imagine what the Fall of China and the bombing of Britain will do!"

Carver whirled and clicked a switch on the panel behind him. The monitors changed to headlines and newscasts from around the world. He read them aloud, " 'China Sinks British Fleet!' . . . 'Brits Nuke Beijing' . . . 'H-Bomb Hits London' . . . I wish we could get another H in there . . . 'New Emperor Takes Power!' "

"Tomorrow's news, today," Bond said.

"Yes, Mr. Bond. I am creating the greatest media empire ever formed by man, and it will live or die based on the programming. I intend to provide that programming. William Randolph Hearst, who was to the U.S. in his day what I am to the world in mine, only started one war. I plan to have a war every two years!"

He spun around and clicked more buttons. The monitors changed again, revealing new headlines. Carver read again, " 'War in the Amazon' . . . we'll call it 'Rumble in the Jungle' in the tabloids . . . 'Revolution in South Africa' . . . 'Russia Invades Ukraine' . . . And for our ten-year anniversary, 'U.S. Civil War—Part Two!' "

"I suppose that would make you the most powerful man in the world," Bond said.

"Most powerful *madman*," Wai Lin said.

"True," Bond said. "I stand corrected."

"Mr. Bond, mad or not, I'm *already* the most powerful man in the world."

"Perhaps. But you're still the son of a whore, a bastard, raised in the gutter. And we all sneer at you."

That got Carver where it hurt. His face went red. He stood up and said, "Will you sneer when the fireball vaporizes Buckingham Palace? Will you sneer when the shock wave mows down your private clubs, your Saville Row, your high-and-mighty banks? Will you sneer when the firestorm roasts those pink-cheeked boys at Harrow?"

"Yes. They might be dead but you'll still be a worthless guttersnipe, no better than this muscle-bound, retarded, psychotic *freak*, this mutant, this—"

Stamper couldn't take it. He lurched forward and Bond and Wai Lin exploded into action. Bond swung her around so that she could extend her arm and grab the letter opener from Stamper's thigh. She deftly pulled it out and jumped over to Gupta, dragging Bond with her. As Stamper reached for Bond, she put the blade up to Gupta's throat.

"Don't!" Carver shouted. Stamper stopped, but Bond kept moving. He clamped his arms around the nearest guard and pulled the man in front of him. The machine gun went off, spraying bullets all over the room. Stamper dived onto Carver, protecting him from the gunfire with his own body as more guards rushed into the office. They started firing at Bond.

"Don't hit Gupta!" Carver shouted.

The guard Bond was using as a human shield was killed by the shots. Behind him, the large picture window looking out at the other skyscrapers was shattered. Once that happened, the shooting stopped. Bond backed slowly up to the shattered window with Wai Lin, who was holding Gupta in front of them with the blade still at his throat.

"Don't just stand there!" Carver shouted to the guards. "Get them!"

Four guards rushed forward, but Bond and Wai Lin shoved Gupta into them, knocking them down. At the same time, the handcuffed couple turned and leaped out of the window.

It would have been a straight drop of fifty stories, but they hit the green construction net, which enmeshed them in its strong, thin plastic web.

"How do we get down now?" Wai Lin asked.

Bond's eyes flicked to the huge banner next to him on the side of the building. They were positioned right at Carver's giant forehead.

"Give me the letter opener," he said. Wai Lin handed it over and he slashed the suspension cable free of the banner, then plunged the letter opener into Elliot Carver's forehead. Bond took hold of Wai Lin with one arm around her waist.

"Hold tight!" he said. She held onto him and wrapped

her legs around his torso. Bond hung from the letter opener with his other hand, then together they rode the blade down through the parting banner. Its ripping fabric controlled their descent. Carver's face divided into half as they reached the bottom. Bond grabbed one side of the halved banner as it fell to the edge of the building, arcing over a high bamboo scaffolding. He let go of the swinging banner and dropped with Wai Lin onto the scaffolding.

Up above in the office, they were all looking out the broken window with amazement. Stamper grunted and then charged from the office with several guards in tow.

"Damn them," Carver muttered.

Bond and Wai Lin made their way down the ladders on the scaffolding, only to meet guards ascending from the street. The couple moved to another ladder, but there were still more guards on the way up. Bond looked around and realized they were surrounded. Next to them was a tall, vertical bamboo support pole. It had been bent back and lodged underneath the top of the scaffolding. He looked over to Wai Lin for her approval. She returned the look doubtfully.

"Ready when you are," he said.

They leaped from the platform and grabbed onto the vertical support pole. It broke free and vaulted them over the street's heavy traffic. They landed in a full rubbish skip as the scaffolding across the street collapsed like a pile of toothpicks. A motorcyclist raced right into the bamboo support pole that was now spanning the street. The rider tumbled as his BMW R1200C Cruiser slid onto its side.

Bond and Wai Lin jumped down from the skip,

astonished to find themselves in one piece. Then bullets ricocheted off the skip behind them—more guards were approaching from across the street. They dived for the motorcycle and pulled it upright.

Wai Lin told the driver in Chinese that they were going to borrow his BMW. Before the man could protest, Bond got on in front, his free hand on the throttle. Wai Lin hopped on the back and reached her free hand around to work the clutch. Bond kick started the bike—but it stalled.

"Clutch!" he called out.

Wai Lin pulled the lever. With bullets ripping up the ground around the tires, they burned rubber and tore off down the street.

Upstairs, Carver was watching the getaway in anger. He shouted into a walkie-talkie, "They're getting away! Send a car! Use the goddamned helicopter!"

Black sedans like the ones used in Hamburg poured out of an underground parking garage in pursuit of the motorcycle.

The BMW R1200C was a heavy piece of machinery, sold on the market as Europe's answer to Harley-Davidson. Its top speed was at least 170 miles per hour, and it was more at home on the track than the streets of Saigon. The BMW was quite striking, with a warm, avant-garde, extravagant ivory colour and a fine line of navy blue edging.

The bike sped down the busy boulevard as the guards in sedans closed ground, following them as they turned into a traffic roundabout the wrong way. Cars screeched and swerved to avoid hitting them, only to crash into other vehicles. Horns blared and drivers shouted. Bond and Wai Lin left mayhem and the sedans in their wake as they turned down an alley. They moved at full speed, only to realize that the alleyway was a dead end, ending at a large house.

"Now what?" Wai Lin asked.

"House call," Bond said.

He revved the engine and roared up the front stairs, ready to blast through the closed front door just as a butler opened it from within. The BMW soared through the door, leaving the shocked butler trembling. It went across the polished floor, upsetting furniture and breaking china, then zoomed up a flight of stairs.

They raced down a hallway on the second floor and through open doors leading to a roof terrace. Bond gunned the bike and leaped off of the roof and onto the flat rooftop of the next building. He kept going, jumping from rooftop to rooftop, weaving around chimneys and under hanging laundry. Guards on the street below fired up at them whenever they got a clear shot.

The rooftops ended at a taller apartment building. The motorcycle kept going, though, through an open back door and into a huge loft. Books and papers scattered as they flew past, heading toward a large picture window at the room's opposite end. Before they reached it, however, the rotors of the Augusta A 109 helicopter carrying two guards rose up in view outside.

Bond skidded around and headed back out onto the roof. The helicopter dropped from sight, waiting for the bike to emerge on the ground level. Bond wasn't going to give them the pleasure.

"Hold on," he said to Wai Lin.

He revved the engine again, then sped back into the

loft. He gunned the bike up to full speed and crashed through the picture window. The BMW flew over the Augusta's blades and landed on the rooftop across the street. Then Bond continued the leapfrogging over the flat roofs, trying to get away. The helicopter appeared above them, bearing down. A guard leaned out and fired on them. Just when the chopper was about to catch up and the bullets could hit their targets, a rooftop gave way. Bond and Wai Lin fell through into the apartment below.

The naked Chinese couple making energetic love on the bed nearly had a mutual heart attack as the motorcycle crashed through the ceiling and down into their bedroom. It then roared out onto the communal balcony.

The balcony ran the length of the long building, divided by bamboo curtains and screens. They raced along, scattering the flimsy furniture and partitions as they went.

"See anything you like?" Bond shouted.

Guards in a sedan on the street spotted them. The driver got a bright idea and pulled in underneath the balcony. He began to drive along the pavement, splintering the balcony's wooden support stilts and collapsing the balcony in its wake. The BMW raced just ahead of the falling structure, but the sedan below was quickly overtaking them. Guards leaned out of both sides of the car, firing up at them.

The end of the balcony loomed up. Bond reached its wooden railing just as the sedan below hit the final support stilt—which was made of concrete. The sedan crashed, its windshield spiderwebbing as the guards inside hit it with full momentum. Bond and Wai Lin burst through the end railing and flew through the air. The cycle landed upright on the edge of an open-air market.

Zooming through, they upset stalls, hit produce, and narrowly missed pedestrians and animals. The helicopter had tracked them, however, and was now swooping down and using its rotor blades to chop market stalls and items behind the speeding cycle. Chickens screeched and fluttered. Civilians screamed and ran. Fruit spilled and rolled all over the ground. The Augusta A 109 was closing ground fast. It was a versatile helicopter that was developed for police use, then modified to perform many varied military roles. Civilian models were available for private use, but Carver had apparently acquired one with gunpower.

Bond and Wai Lin cleared the market and headed onto a street full of what looked like a thousand bicycles. The helicopter peeled off as the motorcycle roared into the middle of the traffic, which suddenly parted. Up ahead were two sedans filled with guards, heading directly toward them. At the last second, Bond and Wai Lin took a sharp, skidding turn and pulled into a long alley-way. The sedans closed ground behind them as they sped toward the alley's end, which opened to a boat-filled river. The cycle soared out and onto a boat that was tied to the dock. From there they jumped to the next boat, and then to the next. The sedans skidded to a halt behind them.

The BMW made it all the way across the river by jumping from boat to boat, then onto shore. They entered a narrow courtyard, where they whipped past a muddy fountain, sailed under a wire hung with washing, and skidded to a stop. It was a dead end. A high wall loomed before them. They turned the motorcycle and cleared the washing line just in time to see the Augusta dropping down into the mouth of the alley. It angled its rotors down near the ground and began to move forward, its whirring blades spanning the narrow courtyard.

"Trapped," Wai Lin said.

"Never," Bond replied.

He looked at the three-foot gap between the blades and the ground. The drying clothes whipped in the air as the helicopter approached. Wai Lin stared at the wire holding the clothes.

"Wait a second!" she cried.

She pulled the wash line down and scooped up a large rock from the ground.

"Okay, go!" she yelled.

Bond charged the helicopter and at the last moment laid the bike sideways, sliding under the helicopter blades. Bond and Wai Lin rolled off of the motorcycle as the chopper passed over their heads. Wai Lin then jumped to her feet and tied the rock to the end of the wire wash line. She twirled it like a sling and sent it into the Augusta's tail rotor. The wire and drying clothes wound into the spinning blades like a ball of twine. The rear rotor jammed with a high-pitched whine as the helicopter destabilized, wobbling from side to side. The blades shattered against the courtyard walls and the helicopter exploded spectacularly. Bond grabbed Wai Lin and dived with her into the dead fountain as shrapnel shot over their heads.

After a moment, they sat up slowly, covered in muck. Bond looked at the helicopter wreckage and then at her. He was impressed.

• • •

They found an outside shower in a colourful alley filled with laundry, screaming children, and various animals. Wai Lin stood with her face upturned to the water, enjoying it. She bent down, rinsing her hair, smiling up at Bond, who was watching and admiring her.

"Would you pass the soap?" she asked.

Bond took a bar of soap from a tin can wired to the shower pipe and handed it to her.

"You were pretty good with that rock," he said.

"It comes from growing up in a rough neighborhood. You were pretty good on that motorcycle."

"That comes from not growing up at all."

She laughed as she lathered her long hair. Bond was pulled close to her, his cuffed hand right next to hers as she shampooed.

"Allow me," he said.

He massaged her hair and the nape of her neck. She moaned appreciatively and faced Bond—and both of her hands were free. Somehow she had managed to pick the lock, using her long hair to conceal the act.

"Your turn," she said.

She slapped her free cuff on the shower pipe and snapped it shut, successfully cuffing Bond to the pipe.

"I'm sorry," she said, "but this is a Chinese problem. Thanks for washing my hair. It was great."

She gathered up some white laundry and began to slip it on.

Bond was stupefied as she gave him a little wave, then left the alley. He stood there a moment, feeling foolish, until he yanked the shower pipe off with brute force, spilling the water everywhere. Still wearing the handcuff on his wrist, he dashed into the street after her.

It was filled with what seemed like hundreds of Vietnamese people—all dressed in white! Which one was Wai Lin?

He moved into the crowd and started searching.

THIRTEEN

Together Again

James Bond jogged through the crowd, looking from side to side at the people around him. The handcuffs hung off one wrist, rattling as he ran.

What did she mean, a "Chinese problem"? It was Britain's problem, too! She wasn't just going to walk away from him like that. Who did she think she was? Just because she was one of the most capable operatives— male or female—he had ever seen, it didn't give her the right to take all of this on alone. Normally Bond would have preferred to work by himself, but he had to admit that he thought the woman was simply incredible. What agility and courage she had! He couldn't let her run away like this. An inner voice told him that he should report in to London as soon as possible and let them know what was going on. It was the louder voice that told him to keep searching for Wai Lin.

Except for a handful of instances, Bond's relationships with women had always been casual and noncommittal.

He thought that he had experienced what others called "love" maybe three or four times in his life. The rest of the time it was purely lust, and in a few extreme cases, perhaps intense infatuation. He never had a problem admitting that his attitudes toward the opposite sex were old-fashioned and even somewhat chauvinistic. M had once said he was a "misogynist" but that simply wasn't true. He adored all women. If there was a fault in that, it was a tendency to place women he liked on pedestals.

Throughout the years, he had been involved with many different women—in his personal and professional lives. He had worked with female operatives from other nations before, and he had always enjoyed the brief affairs with them that seemed to inevitably occur at the ends of missions. After the trysts were over, though, he always went back to England, resumed his bachelor lifestyle, and looked out for the next lady of the moment. Was Wai Lin any different? Why was he jeopardizing the mission to find her?

Bond cursed himself and kept searching. He convinced himself that the key to completing this assignment *was* joining forces with the Chinese girl. Their respective governments might listen to them if they reported Carver's intentions together. If his ulterior motive in finding her was so that he could gaze into her almond-shaped eyes again, perhaps kiss those lips, and then maybe touch her smooth light brown skin—so be it.

Out of the corner of his eye, he noticed one figure in white break off from the crowd and go down a side street. Could that have been her?

Wai Lin replaced her earring as she hurried through the swarm of people on the street, intent on getting to her destination before the *gweilo* caught up with her. She hated doing that to him—he didn't deserve it—but she had her instructions and a duty to perform. She couldn't allow herself to let the handsome secret agent from the West influence her actions in any way. She should get away from him and complete the assignment on her own.

Besides, if she had stayed handcuffed to him any longer, she might not have been able to control her desire for him.

She looked behind and saw him far in the distance, but he stuck out amid all the white-clad Vietnamese like a sore thumb. She grinned slightly, for the sight was a bit humorous. He couldn't see her, though. She turned a corner and went down a narrow lane. It took her another minute to emerge onto a busy street facing a small park. A row of bicycles was parked in a rack on the pavement.

The bicycle was where they had said it would be. It was padlocked to the rack, and she was able to pick the lock by using her earring again. She hopped on it and took off for the safe house.

What was it about the man from the West that intrigued her so much? He was just another *gweilo*—a slang term that Asians often used for Westerners. Yet, in many ways, he was different. The man named Bond was resourceful and brave, and she knew he could be a killer without any hesitation. At the same time, there was something tender about him that appealed to her. Deep within the tough exterior was a man with feelings. She could sense that he would be a kind and generous man—especially in bed.

As she rode toward her destination, Wai Lin thought about what she had seen at Carver's headquarters. General Chang and the so-called Crown Prince were there, waiting for the war to start and finish quickly. They might think that installing Hung as the new emperor of China would be an easy operation, but Wai Lin thought differently. She didn't believe the people would accept a monarch again just like that. That particular part of Carver's plan was misguided. The war, however, was extremely likely and had to be stopped. She bore down on the pedals and rode even faster through the streets.

Ten minutes later, Wai Lin arrived at a bicycle repair shop near the Ben Thanh Market. The market has long been one of Saigon's most famous landmarks, having been in existence since the French occupation. Located on a landfill that was once a swamp, the Ben Thanh Market was a major hub of activity in the center of the city.

Wai Lin entered the bicycle repair shop, underestimating how remarkably efficient Carver's intelligence network really was. Stamper had discovered the front for the Saigon headquarters of the People's External Security Force months ago. Although there was now an official building in Hanoi for China's equivalent of the CIA or MI6, they still maintained this clandestine safe house. Unfortunately, it was safe no longer.

The Vietnamese man watching the building from across the street had been waiting for an hour. He worked for the CMGN security force, but wore no uniform. He stood inconspicuously in an alleyway, wondering if the girl or the man would show up. Sure enough, one of them did. The Chinese girl rode her bicycle up to the front of the shop and got off. As she went inside, the man pulled out a cell phone and punched in the numbers.

He didn't get to complete the call, for a spear-hand chopped his neck from behind. His head snapped to one side and then he collapsed. James Bond took the cell phone, disconnected it, and then frisked the man for a gun. He found a Browning 9mm automatic and pocketed it.

Bond had gambled that the figure he had seen leaving the crowd earlier was Wai Lin. He had sprinted up the alley and spotted her. Using stealth techniques he had learned long ago at a training camp in Canada, he followed her to the park. Once she had got on the bicycle and left, Bond took one of his own and pursued her. When he had ridden up this alley, he noticed the stooge watching her.

Bond hid in a doorway as a black sedan rolled up in front of the repair shop. Six thugs got out of the car; five went inside and one man remained outside to stand guard. Bond moved up the street, then crossed the road so that he could walk along the pavement on the same side of the street as the shop. The guard had a gun in his belt and an unlit cigarette in his mouth. He started to pat down his pockets, looking for a light. Bond walked up to him and helpfully searched his own pockets for matches, but came up empty. He shrugged apologetically, then slammed his fist into the thug's jaw. The man collapsed into a heap on the pavement. Then Bond heard something crash inside the store.

He entered the shop in time to dodge one of the guards flying into the wall. Another guard was on the floor, groaning.

Wai Lin was in the midst of fighting the three other assailants. She was doing so well that Bond had to stop and admire her form. She was literally a dynamo. The men appeared to be martial arts experts themselves, but they were no match for her. Wai Lin took one man by the arm and tossed him over her shoulder into the counter, then turned on the other two with lightning-fast chops and kicks until they were out cold. The first man by the door regained consciousness, got to his feet, and pulled his gun. He came up behind her and stuck it in the back of her head. Wai Lin spun around, but the man cocked the gun and aimed it right at her forehead. He smiled at her as he prepared to squeeze the trigger. She closed her eyes.

Instead of a gunshot, she heard a loud cracking sound. She looked to see the man's eyes rolling up into his head. He fell with a thud, revealing Bond standing behind him with a spear-hand outstretched. Before Wai Lin could react, he slapped the end of the handcuffs on her wrist. They were bound together once more.

"I have a confession to make," he said. "Carver was right. I'm not really a banker. I'm in the British Secret Service."

"I have to admit, Carver was right about me, too," she said.

"It looks as if we're working together after all."

"You really want to be partners?"

"Why not? There have been more mismatched couples." Wai Lin smiled. "All right."

"I'm guessing you have a secure communications link. I'd like to borrow it to report to my chief."

"If I did have such a thing, it would be busy. I'd be reporting to my chief."

"Why don't we just send a joint report?"

"And why don't you just go to your embassy and send your own?"

"Two reasons. First, a joint report would get our chiefs talking to each other, which might be the only way to avoid the war."

"And second?"

"What do you know about stealth technology?"

Wai Lin pulled the earring out of her lobe and used it to unlock both sides of the handcuffs. She tossed them away and replaced the earring.

"I've learned a lot about it lately," she said. "Why?"

"The MiGs were shot down, but not by the *Devonshire*. You saw. The one large cruise missile was missing, but none of the small ones were fired."

"But the MiGs did not see anything on their radar, except your ship."

"And our ship didn't see anything on its radar except the MiGs. But the MiGs didn't sink it, unless you've invented a new torpedo that doesn't explode."

"Not on purpose, anyway," she said and allowed a smile. "Certainly not a torpedo that goes around corners and carefully avoids damaging the missile room."

"It could have come only from some kind of stealth boat."

"Russia has been developing low-emission radars so stealth planes can use radar without giving themselves away. We happened to get one of those. But it was stolen—from one of General Chang's bases. I traced it to Hamburg. That's how we met."

"I'd bet my life that Elliot Carver owns a stealth boat."

"I'd bet my life that he's on his way to it right now."

"You know what I think? I think we have until an hour after dark tonight to find that boat and sink it."

"I think you're right."

Wai Lin turned to press a concealed switch behind the

counter. A rack of bicycles slid away to reveal a high-tech area beyond. There were computers, monitors, telephones, and video cameras. There was also a table and cabinet full of weapons and supplies. Bond busied himself looking at all this while Wai Lin sat at a computer terminal.

"Get us some gear; just don't make any noise," she said. "I have to concentrate on this."

Much of the equipment was straightforward, but some of it was the Chinese equivalent of items that might have been created in Q Branch. Bond picked out a deflated Zodiac boat, dive equipment, two Daewoo .380 automatic pistols, ammunition, and a stack of round, green, magnetic limpet mines. He started making two neat piles—one for himself and one for Wai Lin.

"All right," she said, looking at the monitor. "Of the harbours and inlets controlled by General Chang, twenty-two are in highly populated areas. That leaves fourteen."

"But a stealth boat would only come out at night. It's not invisible, only invisible to radar. Let's assume a top speed of thirty knots. Eight hours of darkness, four hours out, four hours back—they'd have to be within a hundred and twenty miles of where we found the wreck."

Wai Lin went to work with this information. Bond picked up a Chinese fan and opened it. As it unfolded, small knives went flying into the ceiling—*whap! whap! whap!*

Wai Lin gave him a look. "You break it, you buy it."

"Sorry," he said.

She continued to work. Bond's curiosity got the better of him. He examined the objects one by one. There was an interesting umbrella with a blow-dart capability. A bag of rice was marked "Poison" in Chinese characters.

190

A pair of aluminum chopsticks was in actuality two perfectly balanced knives. He tried flinging one across the room. It spun in the air and stuck into the head of a mannequin. Some kind of explosive built into the chopstick went off with a resounding boom two seconds later, demolishing the head.

"I thought I asked you to be quiet," Wai Lin said. Her fingers worked furiously on the keyboard.

Bond picked up a small, ornate music box. Wai Lin sat up and said, "All right, that leaves four places to check—*don't open that box!*"

He froze. "What does it do?"

"It plays 'Memory' from *Cats*. Sorry, it sticks in my head."

Bond nodded in agreement and replaced it carefully. "Now check those four places for anything unusual. Drownings. Fishing accidents."

"All right, but you'd better not touch anything."

"I've learned my lesson," he said.

She started pulling up records but got very short replies. After a moment, though, a long string of Chinese characters filled the screen.

"Look at this. Four missing boats, three unexplained drownings—that has to be it. Ha Long Bay."

Bond frowned. Ha Long Bay was part of North Vietnam.

They spent the next several minutes doing something unprecedented in the history of British and Chinese relations: James Bond and Wai Lin wrote and transmitted a joint intelligence report to their respective superiors. They had both signed the document with their code names.

"Now, why couldn't our two countries have had this

kind of cooperation in the eighteen hundreds?" Bond asked.

"Everyone was too busy smoking opium," she replied.

Bond gathered his equipment and nodded to her pile. It was a standard assortment of goods: Mares wet suits, Dacor twin 100s, regulators, fins, and masks. "Can you think of anything else we might need?"

"Transportation," she said. "I'll call the Orient Express."

Bill Tanner had fallen asleep in his chair in the MI6 office. M was quietly studying the *Devonshire*'s last transmissions in her own office. Most of the staff were home asleep. It wouldn't be dawn for a few more hours.

The soft beeping sound from the transmittal system roused Tanner from dreams of hitting a par three on the fourteenth hole at the Royal St. George's. He was about to curse at the alarm clock when he realized what was making the noise. He leaped to his feet when he saw the signal with the code name "Predator" attached to it. Tanner shouted, "It's Bond!"

M's office door flung open and she came rushing out. Together they looked at the signal as it went through the decoding process.

"My God, he filed it jointly with a Chinese agent," M said softly.

Tanner grinned. "What do you expect? The Chinese agent is female."

They read the report together.

"Well, we were right," she said. "Now if I can convince the buffoons in the situation room that we're right, we just might be able to stop this thing. Come on." She walked over to the coffeemaker and poured two cups. She snapped on two plastic lids and handed one cup to Tanner. She then gestured with her head toward the door.

It was still dark outside as M and her chief of staff left the MI6 building and got into her Rolls-Royce. Tanner was about to offer to drive, but M got behind the wheel herself. He shrugged and got in on the passenger side.

As they pulled out of the drive and headed for Whitehall, she said, "This is it, Tanner," she said. "If we don't win this battle, we'll lose the war."

Elliot Carver, Henry Gupta, and Stamper stood on the dock and inspected the *Sea Dolphin II*, the sleek stealth boat that Carver's scientists had spent two years building in secrecy. The captain was making last-minute preparations to leave the hidden base inside a large rock jutting out of Ha Long Bay.

They had arrived in Carver's seaplane just minutes before. After Bond and Wai Lin had escaped from the Saigon headquarters, the media mogul figured that he had no time to waste. He had seen what the two agents could do, and there was no telling when or how they might pop up again. They knew too much. He wasn't worried, though. He was confident that he and his men would pull off the operation as planned. However, the uncertainty of the two agents' possible interference did not relieve any of the stress. He rubbed the muscles in his jaw and popped three tablets of ibuprofen. The TMJ had gotten worse in the last couple of days. He chalked it up to tension and tried to concentrate on the job at hand.

"Henry," Carver said, "in just a few hours we'll know just how much of a genius you really are."

Gupta chuckled. "Come on, Boss, you already know.

They're going to put my brain in a goddamn museum someday."

"Don't count on it being in the British Museum, Henry." Carver looked at his watch impatiently. He called to the captain, "Hurry up; we only have a few hours until sundown."

"We'll be ready," the captain replied.

Stamper stood by with a machine gun in his hand. Carver turned to him. "What are you doing just standing there? What have you learned about Bond? Anything?"

"No, Boss. He's probably still in Saigon for all we know. Sorry. You want me to call again? I just talked to them ten minutes ago."

"You disappoint me, Stamper," Carver said. "I was going to give you the Chinese girl if you caught them, but now I don't know . . ."

"Oh, please, Mr. Carver, I would really like that," Stamper said. His mouth was watering. "Give me another chance, okay?"

"Well, we hope that we won't see those two again. But if we do, and you are successful in stamping out that British spy and wife thief, perhaps I will give the girl to you as a small reward . . ."

"Oh, you can be sure that I'll get him next time. You just watch."

"Stamper, you were a good lad when I first met you, and you're a good lad now." He smiled lovingly at his henchman, then suddenly barked, *"Don't screw up again!"* Carver then turned back to the captain and told him once again to hurry up.

Stamper watched Carver with admiration. He didn't mind it when the boss yelled at him. He was used to it. Besides, he was working for the most powerful man in the world. That made him the most powerful security officer in the world. He liked the sound of that.

Tonight there would be an enormous amount of death and destruction. They would capture it all on video for the news around the world. Men would die and ships would be blown apart. He would be contributing to the onset of a major war. He was about to be a part of history.

Stamper liked the sound of that, too.

FOURTEEN

Bay of the Descending Dragon

The Vietnamese often call it the "Eighth Wonder of the World."

Ha Long Bay is situated in the northeastern part of Vietnam, 165 kilometers from Hanoi. Its name means the "Bay of the Descending Dragon," referring to an old legend handed down from past generations: Long ago, the gods sent a family of dragons to earth to help defend the people from invading foreigners. The dragons landed on what is now Ha Long Bay, spewing out jewels and jade. When these huge gems hit the water, they turned into the various islands and islets dotting the seascape and created a formidable fortification against the invaders. The people were able to defend themselves and turn away their enemies. Eventually they founded the country of Vietnam. The dragon family had become so fond of the area that they decided to remain on the earth. The dragon mother settled on what is now Ha Long, and the children scattered around Bai Tu Long.

The dragons' tails created the area known as Bach Long Vi, known for the white, sandy beaches of Tra Co peninsula.

As the legend implied, Ha Long Bay is notable for its calm, clear emerald-coloured water and its 1,600 limestone rocks, islands, and islets. Arguably the most beautiful spot in Vietnam, the area has only recently been made available to the West with the advent of *Doi Moi*, the country's policy of opening its economy to foreign trade. Many of the islands are quite large and there are several small alcoves with sandy beaches where swimming is possible. There are also caves and grottoes situated on some of the islands. Hang Dau Go, perhaps the most impressive, is a huge cave of three chambers. Some of the islands have unusual configurations. The most notable are Dinh Huong, which resembles a tripod used as an incense burner; Hon Dua, which appears to be a pair of chopsticks; and Ga Choi, or "fighting cocks."

Wai Lin used her connections with the Chinese government to get them a flight to Hanoi that very day. They hustled to get to the airport and passed through Customs with no problems.

It was late afternoon when they arrived in North Vietnam. They hired a rental car and drove to Ha Long City, the main town in the region. Ha Long City is divided into two halves, one on the mainland and one on a neighbouring island. Traversing the bay required the use of one of the many tourist junks, which could be hired by haggling with the owners at the dock.

They now stood on the hilly shore overlooking the amazing bay. Wai Lin was talking to a Chinese fisherman while Bond scanned the horizon. There were several boats on the water, but nothing looked out of the ordinary.

Wai Lin finished with the fisherman and turned to Bond. "See that island? The far one, there."

She pointed to one way out in the distance.

"He says they all avoid it, that it's dangerous for boats to be around there at sunset. He'll take us, but he wants five thousand American dollars."

Bond frowned. "Will he take a cheque?"

They were able to find an American Express office still open in Ha Long City. Bond used the company credit card, certain that M would approve the expenditure once it was explained.

"We had better eat, don't you think? I'm starving," Wai Lin said.

"We have a couple of hours before sunset. Yes, let's," Bond said. "We'll need our strength."

They went into a small restaurant in the city and ordered a traditional Vietnamese meal. The cooking in the country is usually not as rich or heavy as the coconut milk curries of India or Thailand. Seafood is a major staple of the diet, of course, as Vietnam has an extensive coastline.

Bond and Wai Lin shared *pho bo,* a soup made from a rich beef broth containing beef strips and *banh pho* noodles. A mainstay of Vietnam, *banh pho* are wide white rice stick noodles briefly boiled in salted water. They also had *ga xoi mo,* deep-fried chicken with a marinade made from an abundance of spices. The main dish was *bo nhung dam,* which began as very thin slices of raw beef and onions dipped into a simmering beef broth. The cooked meat was then rolled into a rice paper bundle with fresh basil, mint, cilantro, carrots, bean sprouts, cucumber, and lime. The rolls were dipped in *nuoc nam* and *nuoc cham* for more flavour. There were no alcoholic beverages, so they both drank sodas with their meals. As they had not eaten all day, the food was extremely satisfying.

After they finished their meal, they hurried back to the fisherman, paid him, and set off in his fishing junk. Many of the junks were motorized now to take advantage of the expanding tourist trade.

They sailed out into the beautiful bay as the sun was going down. The golden-red light reflected off of the water, casting a magical glow around the formations. Bond and Wai Lin sat on the bow of the boat while the fisherman stayed in the back controlling the rudder. The day had been an unusually long one. Bond found it difficult to believe that he had begun it in Japan, spent part of the day in Saigon, and was now in North Vietnam.

They were silent for several minutes, enjoying the scenery. Bond finally asked, "How did a girl like you get to be in the secret service?"

She shrugged. "It's mostly dull routine, of course. But one of the two reasons I joined was that it would be more like this—sailing through a beautiful evening with a dangerous mission ahead, forced to partner with a decadent but handsome agent of a corrupt Western power."

Bond laughed and said, "And they say Communists don't know how to have fun."

"Yes, I hate that stereotype. The serious Chinese Communist in the glasses and tunic. Look at me, I don't even have a little red book."

"And the second reason?"

She hesitated, then looked at Bond. "Well, I wanted to

find a job where there was a chance of meeting people who don't find strong or sexually aggressive women to be threatening." Then she grinned.

Wai Lin had put the idea on the table—now it was up to him. Bond said, "Well, I think you picked the right line of work. And if I may say so, you picked the right decadent, corrupt Western agent as a partner."

With that, he leaned closer and kissed her. She put her arms around him and they kissed longer and more intimately. Then they began to sink down onto a billowy spare sail at their feet. She wrapped her legs around him and they snuggled together for the few precious minutes before they had to face the dangerous tasks ahead of them. They pulled the sail over their bodies for privacy.

They thought perhaps it might be the last night they would be together, or even possibly the last night they would be alive. They made love with an intensity and passion that burned their loins and made their hearts race. For a half hour they were oblivious to the outside world, lost in each other's desire. When their bodies joined, they experienced a much needed, satisfying catharsis. She clawed his back as she reached a climax quickly, muffling her cries against his bare shoulder.

The denouement of their lovemaking brought the dusk. They emerged from the covers and composed themselves. The fisherman paid no attention to them. He glanced around nervously, obviously afraid of whatever it was that was "out there." Bond and Wai Lin dressed in their wet suits and prepared the other equipment.

Bond inflated the Zodiac raft and cast it into the water. He and Wai Lin climbed down a rope ladder and boarded it, then waved good-bye to the fisherman. The junk sailed toward home, and Bond steered the Zodiac toward the mysterious island the man had told them about.

They waited another half hour, until the sun had completely set. The stars were out in force, and the island was a mere silhouette against the moonlit sea.

"Look," Wai Lin said, pointing.

Pinpricks of artificial light suddenly popped on in an area at the base of the island.

"That looks like some kind of natural cove," Bond said.

He gunned the Zodiac and headed for it.

"There's something moving in front of it," Wai Lin said.

Bond saw a large, shadowy shape slide over the lights, obscuring them. As they got closer, they could see that it was indeed another vessel of some kind. The *Sea Dolphin II* had emerged from its hiding place and was headed straight out to sea.

Bond angled the Zodiac so that it was right in the path of the stealth boat. In moments, it was looming over them. Bond thought it looked like some kind of futuristic machine from a science-fiction film—its design was sleek, high-tech, and menacing. The two of them were silent as the craft silently enveloped them. Their little boat sailed directly beneath the platform area between the two pontoons, dwarfed by the behemoth that Elliot Carver and his men had created.

Bond swung a grappling hook at the side of the starboard pontoon. When it caught, Wai Lin tied the boat to the pontoon. Bond retrieved the grappling hook just as the stealth boat started to pick up speed.

"We caught it just in time," Wai Lin said. She gathered

the limpet mines they had brought and distributed them. They didn't need the aqualungs after all.

"The fuses are set for twenty minutes, but we should be out of here in five. I'll take the other pontoon," Bond said.

He looked up and saw that she was smiling at him.

"What's funny?" he asked.

"You're suddenly all protective. I've blown up bigger boats than this by myself."

"And just think: Only a few years ago, women could be arrested if they tried to blow up boats by themselves," he quipped.

With the mines tied around her waist, Wai Lin jumped up and caught an overhead stanchion. "I'll take the other pontoon," she said. She proceeded to cross the water by climbing hand over hand. She looked like an acrobat in a circus. When she got to the pontoon, Bond blew her a kiss.

Inside the bridge of the stealth boat, Elliot Carver was nervously watching the radar displays beside the captain. Stamper stood behind them, ready to jump at his master's whim.

The captain said, "The Chinese squadron is staying aggressively close to the six British frigates, which are still looking in the wrong place for their missing ship."

"Take us right between the two fleets," Carver ordered. "Full speed."

A security officer was watching monitors that were receiving signals from video cameras located around the ship. He had been up for more than twenty-four hours—they all had—preparing for this job. He rubbed his eyes just as Bond's silhouette moved, unseen by him, across

203

one of the monitors. Fortunately, the cameras didn't pick up the Zodiac boat.

Within minutes, the stealth ship was in position.

Carver looked at his watch. It was time. His moment had arrived. Everything he had worked for had finally come to this.

"Right, let's get started," Carver said. "Fire one missile at the flagship of each fleet. Make sure they miss, but not by much."

Bond was busy on his pontoon placing a limpet mine. At the same time he was thinking how they might make their escape once the fireworks started. The Zodiac wasn't very fast. If the crew of the stealth boat detected their presence, or if they saw them trying to sail away as the limpet mines were blowing, he and Wai Lin might be sitting ducks. He could only hope that they would be successful in keeping quiet and out of sight until they could slip away in the dark.

A deafening noise startled him and he felt a blast of heat just a few feet away. The first missile went off and shot into the night sky. He looked over at Wai Lin. The second missile shot off from her pontoon and she reacted to it. Her eyes met Bond's and again they read each other's thoughts: it was beginning; they had to hurry. She grabbed her mines and ran toward the bow of the ship.

The British fleet's flagship, HMS *Bedford*, was another type 23 Duke class frigate armed with SAS and SAM missiles. Admiral Kelly stood with the captain of the ship in the operations room watching the various consoles. So far the Chinese fleet had not made any threatening noises, but they were getting a little too close for comfort.

Kelly was a sensible man, but he was also patriotic and extremely loyal. He would do what needed to be done to defend his fleet and stand up to China for the sake of Great Britain. The captain shared the admiral's enthusiasm, but not the man's years of experience. Still, the Royal Navy could do no better than having Captain James McMahon at the helm of the flagship.

Suddenly, the leading seaman's monitors flashed.

"Missile inbound," he called. "Bearing two-forty. Range fifteen miles."

The captain immediately turned to his PWO—principal warfare officer—a lieutenant commander.

"Pee-woe, increase to maximum speed, come hard left, thirty degrees," he commanded. "Pee-woe" was naval slang for the PWO.

Admiral Kelly turned to another sailor and said, "Yeoman, tell all ships to alter to antimissile defensive course." To the staff operations officer, he said, "Send a signal to the Admiralty: 'Task Group under missile attack.'"

The leading seaman said, "Range ten miles. Bearing two-forty."

The captain looked at Admiral Kelly. Kelly gave him a reassuring nod and said, "They've thrown down the glove. If it's a fight they want, by God, we'll give them one."

The *Bedford* took evasive action and zigzagged at a very high speed. The missile came closer . . . closer . . . then streaked past the ship and exploded in the water just beyond it. In the operations room, everyone breathed a sigh of relief.

The captain then reported, "Their fleet's turning toward us, sir."

Admiral Kelly looked at the monitors and made a decision.

He said, "They expect us to back down, but they'll be disappointed. Turn the task group towards *them*. Fire one Harpoon. Warning shot. But part their hair with it."

The captain issued the orders and they were transmitted to the other five ships in the fleet.

Bond picked up his speed, knowing the missile would reach its target any minute. He hoped that the frigate would outmaneuver it, as the ship was perfectly capable of doing so at that range. He climbed onto one of the supports of the starboard pontoon and planted a mine in a spot that might easily be found. The support was something like a flying buttress. He then reached around the support and placed a second mine behind the first. Bond figured that a guard making a very careful search would be satisfied with finding the first mine. He continued planting the mines along the pontoon and almost stepped into the view of a rotating video camera. He ducked back just in time. He looked over to the other pontoon to warn Wai Lin about the cameras, but he didn't see her.

He couldn't worry about her now. She knew the score. He concentrated on finishing the task at hand.

The captain of the *Sea Dolphin II* monitored the Royal Navy's actions and reported, "Each fleet has responded to our missiles by firing one missile of their own."

Carver asked, "Only one? Admirable restraint. No pun intended."

The captain and Stamper looked at him blankly.

"Admirable?" Carver said again. "Admiral? Oh, forget it. Well, we'll heat things up, in—*God damn you all! Are you blind!*"

Everyone froze. They had no idea what had caused his sudden outburst.

"What the hell do I pay you for?" With that, Carver strode over to the security console. He grabbed the hair of the exhausted crew member stationed there and pointed his head at one of the monitors. The camera covered the center area of the portside pontoon. The monitor showed nothing in particular, so the frightened crew member gave his boss a questioning glance.

"The camera is rotating, you worthless, contemptible, subhuman cretin!" Carver shouted. "Put it on manual! Rotate it back!"

Awkwardly, because Carver still held him by the hair, the crew member rotated the camera until the camera revealed a profile of Wai Lin. She was unaware that she had been spotted.

Carver glared at the monitor, then said to Stamper, "Hit him."

Stamper reacted immediately to the order and slammed the hapless crew member with a bone-crushing right. Carver was left with bits of the man's hair between his fingers. He shook the strands free.

"If she's there, Bond is there. Find them and kill them," he said.

Stamper raced out to obey. Carver looked down at the moaning man at his feet, then gave an order to another guard, "Dump this man overboard."

With that, Carver turned on his heels and stormed through the double doors that led to his private quarters.

The guards immediately grabbed hold of the crewman and pulled him up and outside. "No! No!" he cried, but he quickly learned that the price of failure was more than a bad annual performance review.

Wai Lin planted her last mine on the portside pontoon. It was done. Now she had to find James and get the hell off the boat. She straightened up from her crouch and, as swiftly as a frog snatching a fly with its tongue, Stamper's hand suddenly fastened on her back and pulled her through a hatch and into the ship.

They were in an access area numbered 4, a small room containing nothing but a ladder and the hatches to the outside and to the rest of the ship. Stamper held Wai Lin firmly by the waist. She struggled like a wildcat, but the German was not bothered. He gave orders to four guards carrying MP5K submachine guns.

"Get out there and shoot him. Be careful, he's tricky. I'll send other men down to help you find the mines."

They saluted him and went one by one out the hatch. Stamper had never been saluted before. He liked it.

"Let's go, baby," he said to Wai Lin, and pulled her out of the access area toward the bowels of the ship. He hoped that Carver would keep his promise and allow him to keep the girl. His mind started reeling with the possibilities of what he might do . . .

Outside, James Bond came around one of the starboard pontoon supports and nearly collided with one of the guards, who was just as startled as Bond. The man brought up his MP5K but 007 was quicker. He backhanded the guard with his silenced pistol, knocking him into the turbulent water.

Bond ducked back into the alcove as a burst of submachine gunfire ripped past him. There was a second guard behind the one he had knocked into the water. Out of the corner of his eye, he saw two guards on the other pontoon aiming their weapons at him. He smoothly extended his hand with the gun, fired two silenced shots, and hit them before they could fire. They fell into the water, dead.

Without pausing, Bond swung back out and snapped off a shot that caught the second guard right in the throat. The man choked and gargled for a second, then fell into the water and vanished instantly. Bond dived into the next alcove, but as soon as he got there, a hatch right in front of him started to open. He jumped onto it, so that he was hanging on behind it when it swung open.

Three guards came out of the hatch. Two of them joined the hunt for Bond while the other one stayed. Now alone, that guard felt the jab of Bond's pistol on the back of his neck. With his other hand, Bond removed his shoulder pack and put it on the guard. He then brutally pushed the guard forward in sight of his fellow thugs. The other two men saw the shape in a black shirt wearing the distinctive pack, and they opened fire. The guard's body hit the water and disappeared before anyone could realize it wasn't the British secret agent.

Bond ducked through the hatch, which was to access area number 2. He shut the door, then climbed up the ladder. He knew now that they probably had Wai Lin.

Elliot Carver sat at the desk in his private quarters. A spiral staircase led up into it from the bridge. He was facing a wall of video monitors duplicating the bank of viewscreens on the bridge of the stealth ship. There were additional monitors broadcasting the various newscasts and headlines of his media empire. Henry Gupta sat nearby, nervously twisting his beard. Carver rubbed his jaw. The pain was worse than ever.

The intercom buzzed. Carver picked it up and heard the news that Bond had been shot and that his body had fallen into the sea.

"You're sure? Good. Now find the mines. Where's Stamper?"

On cue, Stamper came into the room via the spiral staircase with Wai Lin still kicking and struggling.

Gupta said, "Talk about 'speak of the devil.'"

Carver said, "Never mind," and shut off the intercom.

Stamper approached Carver like a teenage boy asking to borrow Dad's new Corvette.

"I know you said to kill her, but before, you said I could keep her," Stamper murmured. "I promise, she won't be any trouble—"

"I'll show you trouble, you—" Wai Lin spat.

She thrust her knee into Stamper's groin. Both Carver and Gupta winced, but Stamper didn't flinch.

"That tickled!" he said with a grin.

Then he slapped her hard on the side of the head, knocking her unconscious. Her body fell to the floor like a rag doll.

"Sir?" he asked. "Please? I'll videotape everything, of course."

"Very well," Carver said. "You can keep her."

Three guards came into the room, responding to Carver's signal.

"Put her in irons, then deliver her to Stamper's room," he told them.

"Thank you, thank you!" Stamper gushed.

"But first, the mines," Carver said sternly, like a father teaching a young son to do his chores before watching television.

"Yes, sir!"

Stamper handed Wai Lin over to the guards and ran back down the spiral stairs. Wai Lin began to stir and the guards covered her with their MP5Ks.

Gupta asked, "How come you're always giving presents to Psycho-kraut?" He thought that *he* should be thrown a bone every once in a while.

"That one would give you a heart attack," Carver said, referring to the Chinese girl.

"I can handle her!" Gupta winked at her and blew a kiss.

Wai Lin glared at him with hatred in her eyes but said nothing.

Back in the operations room of HMS *Bedford,* the air warfare officer pulled off his headset and shouted, "Sir! AWACS reports two waves of land-based MiG-21s inbound. The first group should be on our screens in two minutes!"

Admiral Kelly responded, "Yeoman, tell all ships: 'Air threat warning Red.' "

If there was going to be a war, then it was imminent.

FIFTEEN

Crisis Time

Everyone in the situation room at the Ministry of Defence in London had remained on active duty ever since M and her team stormed out of the room two days ago. A crisis brought out the best and worst in people, and sometimes tensions could erupt due to misunderstandings, bruised egos, and pure stubbornness. Keeping calm, cool, and collected during such a situation was an admirable trait, and even Bill Tanner was amazed that M could remain so. She had taken an immense amount of abuse from the senior male members of the Task Force, yet she had persevered with her belief that all was not what it seemed.

The next day she had arrived at the Ministry of Defence in the morning and was asked to meet privately with the minister of defence. She was barred from the situation room and ordered to remain at her office at MI6 until she "was needed." M was insulted and humiliated, but perceived that the minister himself had been against this course of action and had been pressured by others. M and Tanner went back to MI6 headquarters, and the men continued to look at monitors and wait.

At around the same time that Bond and Wai Lin started planting limpet mines on Elliot Carver's stealth ship several time zones ahead, the dawn found the situation room in a sad, silent state. No news was bad news.

They were supposed to be men of action, yet for the last sixteen hours they had done nothing but stare blankly and helplessly at the viewscreens with little or no suggestion about what they should do. The minister felt frustrated and frightened. He knew that without M in the large room, only the truly perceptive would have noticed that a certain dynamic was missing from the equation. He was aware of it, but wasn't sure if the first sea lord, standing next to him at the monitors, would have perceived it. A dozen other senior naval officers, including Admiral Roebuck, stood behind them. The minister was probably the only one who missed M's presence.

Then reports from HMS *Bedford* started coming in. Missile attacks, MiGs . . . The situation room came alive and the men huddled even farther into the monitors. They were still completely helpless and could only listen and pray.

A staff officer announced, "MiGs are eight minutes from missile firing range."

The quiet tension was interrupted by sounds of shouts and commotion at the door. The officers turned to stare as M burst into the room, followed by Tanner and trailed by two military policemen who had drawn their sidearms. They were clearly reluctant to open fire on a senior government official in a Sonya Rykiel suit.

The minister of defence grimaced and said, "Really, M, you can't just—"

"Listen to me!" she said, cutting him off. "Our agent 007 and a Chinese agent have sent a joint report to the head of the Chinese Secret Service and to me."

Tanner started passing out copies to everyone.

She continued, "Tell your ships to search for a ship that's invisible, or almost invisible, to radar—"

"A *joint* report?" Admiral Roebuck exclaimed. "Your agent, giving aid to the enemy?"

"The Chinese are not the enemy," M said. "It's exactly that kind of thinking that's brought us to the brink of war. You gentlemen, and your counterparts in China, are being played like violins!"

With perplexed looks on their faces, the men read the pieces of paper in their hands.

Stamper's guards moved carefully around the pontoons on both sides of the stealth boat, cautiously searching for the limpet mines that Bond and Wai Lin had placed. One by one, they were gingerly collected and thrown into the water.

Stamper himself joined the search. He might not have been the brightest man in the world, but he had good instincts. He could smell trouble, and sometimes he had a sixth sense for it.

He was searching around a support where he suspected Bond might have placed a mine. Sure enough, it was there. Stamper removed it and tossed it into the water, then he started to move on. That sixth sense must have kicked in, for he slowly turned back to the support. He climbed up and reached around, putting his fingers on the second mine Bond had placed as a backup to the first.

Feeling proud of himself, he pulled it off and threw it into the sea. The boss would be proud.

He wished he could have found the Englishman. Just being shot and thrown into the ocean was not good enough for him. He would have killed him *good,* Stamper thought. The spy had been trying to screw up the boss's plans. Screwing up the boss's plans meant screwing up Stamper's plans. That he didn't like.

At least there was the girl. The boss had promised her to him. That was some consolation. He would do to her what he would have done to Bond, only it would be a lot more fun. He couldn't wait to be finished with the damned mines.

With his sixth sense sharply attuned, Stamper moved on and continued the search.

Elliot Carver paced up and down in his private office, while Henry Gupta worked furiously on the controls of the computer.

"How long?" Carver asked. "One side or the other is going to start the war in five minutes."

"We're feeding the targeting data in now," Gupta said. "Seconds away."

"Good." He pressed another intercom button. "Captain, get us into firing position and bring us to a stop."

Carver rubbed his jaw, but for the first time in a long while he was too excited to feel the pain. All of the news items reporting the war had already been written by computer. They had been constructed so that several variations of the story, depending on the actual details of the event, could be transmitted at the touch of a button. No matter how the battle turned out, Carver was ready with the "correct" version of the facts. In a short while, the Carver Media Group Network would make history as the only communications organization to report live the outbreak of a war.

It had been years since Carver felt this great. He was as high as a kite and just as irrational.

Deeper within the ship, James Bond was on a lower catwalk near the bulkhead. He flattened himself against the wall to keep from being seen by three guards on the catwalk up ahead. He checked the magazine of his silenced pistol. Damn, only two bullets left. He pulled a combat knife from the sheath on his shin and got ready to make his move.

The three guards were in mid-conversation, pleased that they hadn't been given the order to go out and search for the limpet mines. They were expecting a big payoff later that night if the boss's plan went well. It was all they cared about.

"Me," one said, "I'm going to take the money and go to an island somewhere."

"I'm going to my favourite brothel," another said.

"Why spend it?" the practical one asked. "A penny saved is a penny—*Eeigghh!*"

Bond had abruptly changed the subject by sliding the combat knife into the guard's solar plexus with one hand, while shooting the other two neatly in their foreheads with the other. Hearing a noise behind him, Bond whirled around and hurled the bloody knife into the chest of another guard who had just stepped up onto the catwalk. It was all over and silent in two seconds. Bond retrieved the knife and wiped the blood on the man's shirt.

A roll of duct tape was sitting on the catwalk. Bond

looked at it and got an idea. He picked it up and shoved it in his pocket.

He stopped a moment to get his bearings. What had happened to Wai Lin? Had they got her?

He continued moving forward through the ship, formulating a new plan that might stop Carver's insane scheme without Bond's having to kill the enemy one by one until he found the madman and forced him to stop. If he found Wai Lin along the way, so much the better.

In the operations room of HMS *Bedford,* the principle warfare officer reported, "Sir, the MiGs are still one minute away from missile range, but they've just turned on their targeting radar." Captain McMahon nodded in acknowledgment.

Admiral Kelly put forth his view on the matter. "Captain, we might not be able to hold off that many planes, but I'm damned if we'll go to the bottom alone. Tell all ships, as soon as the first MiG fires, they're to fire everything they've got at the Chinese fleet."

"Yes, sir," the captain said.

The yeoman stood up and said loudly, "Urgent message from the Admiralty, sir!" He tore off a long sheet from his printer and handed it to the admiral. He read it, then read it again to make sure he was seeing correctly. He handed the long signal to the captain. "Look at this," he said. "They've gone mad."

He stepped over to the PWO with a concerned look on his face. "Do you have anything on radar that seems very small? Like a lifeboat, a periscope, anything?"

The sailor looked. "No, sir."

The captain looked up from reading the report. He was astonished. "A stealth boat, sir? They *have* gone mad."

The perplexed men huddled around the monitor and searched it for anything, even the tiniest dot.

Not far away, the *Sea Dolphin II* reached firing position and slowed down to a stop. It sat there in the moonlight, a shadow bobbing on the water. It might have been a whale quietly sleeping on the surface.

A lone guard patrolled the work platform at the stern. It was a locker room of sorts where tools and supplies were stored. Some cans of spray paint were rolling in front of a locker. Suspicious, the guard leveled his MP5K and crept over to them. He counted to three, then flung the locker open. He was surprised to see two other guards bound and gagged inside.

The man just had time to register this information when he was struck on the back of the neck by the hard edge of a right hand trained to break boards with a single chop. The man dropped to his knees, and James Bond plucked the Heckler & Koch submachine gun from his nerveless fingers before delivering another well-placed chop on the neck. The guard collapsed, unconscious, across the knees of the two other men. Bond shut the locker on all three of them, then picked up the spray paint cans. He was amassing quite a collection of objects.

Moving on, he soon reached the highest level in the ship. Bond silently stepped onto the stern platform and leaned against a heavy piece of machinery. He had found what he was looking for.

If he leaned over the edge of the platform and looked below at the open area to the rear of the ship, he had a clear view of the cruise missile. It was encased in a heavy steel launch tube that ran parallel to the sides of the stealth boat. There wasn't a guard in sight.

Bond sat down and gathered the odds and ends he had collected—the duct tape, the spray paint cans, a metal canister filled with gasoline—in front of him. Feverishly, he started pulling tape and ripping it as quietly as possible. After he had several pieces, he started taping the cans to the gasoline.

He leaned over to see if anyone had appeared below. A crew member was walking down the catwalk toward the missile. He was unarmed.

Bond picked up the MP5K and switched it to the single-shot mode. He aimed at the inch of catwalk directly in front of the man's right shoe. The shot rang out, the bullet ricocheting off the metal catwalk. The crew member wasn't exactly sure what had just happened. He looked around, then hesitantly took another step. Bond let off another shot, this time a quarter-inch from the man's left foot.

That did the trick. The man turned and fled.

Bond went back to work without further distraction for another two minutes.

On the other side of the world, the Task Force waited anxiously in the situation room for news from the fleet. Tanner kept an eye on M. He could tell she was nervous, but he was the only one who could see that. To the others, she seemed to remain so sure of herself that it frightened them. Because he had got to know her so well over the last couple of years, though, Tanner was able to peer beneath her steely exterior. He didn't blame her for being anxious. Her career was on the line.

The staff officer reported, "Sir, Admiral Kelly reports there is no sign of any stealth boat and—"

"Of course!" M interrupted. "That's the point."

"—he can't stop to look for it; he expects to be fired upon in one minute."

"You must tell him not to fire back," M said.

"I could never order a British fleet not to defend itself," the minister of defence said determinedly.

"Then God help us" was all M could say to that.

Upstairs, in Carver's room, the intercom buzzed.

Gupta triumphantly gave a big sigh. He sat back in his chair, folded his arms across his chest, and smiled. Carver clenched his jaw and ground his teeth.

"Well?" Carver asked.

"All done," Gupta said, as if it wasn't a big deal.

"Good. Get it ready."

The phone buzzed. Stamper's presence was needed immediately at the missile platform for an emergency. Carver demanded to know what was going on.

"What do you mean, there's a sniper?" he shouted into the microphone. "Oh, never mind, I'm coming down myself."

Grumbling, he hurried there with Gupta and found the place covered with guards.

"What the hell is going on?" Carver demanded to know.

"We get shot at when we go out there. I couldn't get to the locks," a crew member said, pointing to the platform by the missile.

"What locks?" Carver asked.

Gupta explained, "When we're at sea, the launch tube is locked down. We can't launch unless someone goes down there and unlatches the launching mechanism."

Carver's eyes narrowed. He grabbed a phone off the

wall and called into it, "Stamper! Get up here and bring the girl! Bond is still alive."

He slammed down the phone and glared at the other men. Then he pushed through the crew members and stepped out onto the platform.

There was nothing in sight.

"Bond?" he shouted. His voice echoed through the chamber.

James Bond looked up from the sculpture he was making and pointed his gun at Carver.

"You won't shoot me, Bond. I've got the girl, you know. Stamper will do what he does best to her if you kill me now. So give it up. The news is already written. The story's already gone to press. There will be no extra editions tonight. If you give up now and hand over your weapon, I'll make sure that Stamper doesn't torture you and the girl. I'll see to it that you'll die quickly and painlessly."

Bond answered him by blasting the catwalk with several bullets, forcing Carver to jump back in fright.

HMS *Bedford* sped toward the Chinese fleet. An automatic alarm started to sound at one of the consoles in the operations room. It was the alarm that all naval personnel dreaded hearing.

"Sir!" the PWO cried. "MiGs are in range. We've been picked up by their targeting radars."

The admiral looked at the captain. They silently acknowledged each other.

"All ships are ready to fire, sir," the captain said. "They'll fire the instant the enemy fires."

They watched the monitors and waited. The palms of their hands were wet and clammy.

Admiral Kelly looked at the radar once again, trying to find whatever it was the Admiralty was talking about.

Bond climbed up on top of the big piece of machinery that had served as his sniper's nest. From up there he could reach the very top of the stealth ship. He used the duct tape to fasten his contraption against the inner surface of the hull. He made sure it was secure, then started to climb down. A noise on the catwalk below stopped him—heavy footsteps. He jumped down to his sniper position and raised the gun to fire again.

It was Wai Lin. Her handcuffs in front were chained to ankle cuffs. Stamper was behind her, using her as a human shield.

"Shoot! Shoot!" Wai Lin cried. "They'll kill me anyway!"

Bond sized up the situation. He looked at his contraption on the ceiling. Then he quickly measured how many feet it was from where he was standing to the railing. Next he determined how far it was from Wai Lin and the railing in front of her and decided it was close enough.

He shouted something in Danish so that Wai Lin could hear him.

Down on the forward platform, Carver heard him and gritted his teeth. "Stamper! Watch out! He's going to try something!"

Bond raised his gun and pointed it upward. Then he counted in Danish, "Three . . . two . . . one!"

He fired at the homemade bomb he had taped to the ceiling. It exploded with a huge noise, blowing a chunk out of the outer hull. At the same instant, Bond performed a neat dive off of his post into the water between the pontoons. Wai Lin simultaneously launched herself straight up and over the catwalk railing, taking advantage of Stamper being distracted by the explosion. Stamper, however, was too fast. He reacted quickly and grabbed Wai Lin's ankle chains before she could disappear over the edge. He slowly pulled her up and back onto the catwalk.

The guards opened fire at Bond. He dived and swam deeper and deeper as the bullets hit the water around him. He had to get to the exterior of the boat now. He couldn't afford to wait for Wai Lin to catch up. She could make it.

Bond swam hard until he got out from under the boat. He broke the surface with a huge gasp of air. He looked up and saw that he was about five yards from the stern of the stealth ship. Wai Lin wasn't there, nor did she appear on the surface after him.

She didn't make it. Now what? he thought. He couldn't just leave her in there.

He felt a sudden surge of rage, then swam toward the boat. He got a very tenuous handhold on the smooth contours of the stern and climbed up.

The PWO on the *Bedford* looked up from his radar screen, astonished. "Sir! We have a new target on the scope, bearing 112 degrees. Very weak signal, can't get the range exactly, but I swear it wasn't there a second ago, sir."

Kelly bent down to look at the radar himself. Sure enough, there was a small blip. It was a ship of some kind.

"Yeoman!" the Admiral called. "Tell all ships: 'Do not fire, repeat do not fire for any reason whatsoever. All ships, turn off weapon system radars and slow to ten knots.'"

"What the hell is it?" the captain asked.

"I don't know—but I don't think they're crazy in London anymore. Yeoman, alert the Admiralty we've spotted something. Then send a message, in the clear, to the Chinese fleet commander: 'Have sighted unknown ship bearing 110 degrees from our position. We would rather fire on it than fire on you.'"

The *Bedford* slowed to ten knots as Chinese MiGs screamed overhead.

Carver and Gupta ran down the catwalk and looked at the top of their ship. They could see stars through the gaping hole in the ceiling.

"The hull's been breached. We can be seen by enemy radar," Gupta said.

The enormity of what Gupta said made Carver's heart miss a beat. He took hold of the intercom and said, "Get us out of here, fast!"

He was furious. He stood on the forward platform and barked orders. "Stamper! Take as many men as you need and get that hole patched." To the guards holding Wai Lin, he said, "Drop her in the ocean. Don't take chances. Shoot her first."

One guard raised his gun and pointed at Wai Lin's head.

"Not here, you idiot," Carver said. "Take her down to the bottom level."

The men brutally yanked her up by the handcuffs and shoved her toward the stairs.

Carver gestured to Gupta and said, "Come on," then left the area.

It was never more silent and tense in the situation room in London.

The news from Admiral Kelly had changed things. There *was* something else in the water there besides the Chinese and British fleets. The minister of defence looked at M. He was now convinced she was right and he hoped they could prove it.

"Sir," the staff officer reported, "the MiGs have turned off their weapons radars. They are climbing to a normal cruising altitude and are on a course for their base."

The Chinese were turning back!

"Admiral Kelly would like to blow that ship out of the water and wonders if you have any objections?" the staff officer said.

Oddly enough, everyone in the room turned to M for her opinion. M looked at Admiral Roebuck and indicated that this one was up to him.

He studied the faces of the others, unsure of what to do, until his eyes rested on M. She gave him a slight nod.

"Send this message to the *Bedford*," Roebuck said. "'Blow it straight to hell.'"

The minister of defence sat down in relief. He picked up a phone and asked for the Prime Minister.

Admiral Roebuck sheepishly approached M and extended his hand. She took it, but she was a little surprised by his old-fashioned gesture: he bowed and lifted her hand to his lips.

In the operations room of the *Bedford*, the automatic targeting alarms stopped sounding, and the officers and men could also breathe a little better. Some of them were shaking hands.

"Admiral, sir, a signal from the Chinese fleet commander," reported the yeoman.

The captain grabbed it and started to hand it to Kelly, but the admiral gestured that the captain should read it.

"To Commander Royal Navy Task Group: We also have the unknown ship on our screens. We will not fire unless it turns toward China. Until then, she's yours. Good hunting."

The admiral responded, "Yeoman, signal the Chinese commander: 'Thank you, sir.' Captain, whatever the hell that thing is, sink it."

"Right, sir." The captain asked the PWO, "That echo is too weak for missile lock?"

"Yes, sir."

"Increase revs to maximum, and load the 4.5 with star shell and H.E. We'll do it the old-fashioned way."

A moment later, the 4.5-inch gun in the bow of the *Bedford* fired a single shot as flame erupted from its muzzle.

Carver and Gupta made it to the bridge in time for the captain to say, "The British have turned toward us. Their flagship is only ten miles away."

"But that's the beauty of stealth," Gupta said. "As soon as we patch that hole, they won't be able to see us anymore."

The 4.5-inch star shell burst high above the stealth boat. It was like a shot from a flare gun, but thousands of times more powerful.

Carver, reacting to the light in the sky, turned to Gupta and said, "You were saying?" To the captain he ordered, "Fire at them!"

"At the British Navy, sir?" the captain asked.

"You heard me!"

A loud explosion rocked the boat. Now that they were

227

visible, the 4.5-inch gun on the *Bedford* started rapidly pumping high explosive shells at them.

The blinding white light revealed the *Sea Dolphin II* vividly. Even Bond was astonished at how huge and naked the stealth ship looked in this light. Now that he could see, he was able to climb much faster.

Bond had a tough time just holding onto, much less climbing up, the speeding, zigzagging ship. He focused on the light coming from the hole he had made in the hull at the top of the boat and headed for that. Then a shell exploded in the water just behind the ship, drenching him with a wave. A minute later, two streaks of flame shot out of the guns over the pontoons as the stealth boat fired a pair of its anti-ship missiles. Bond instinctively ducked as the boat fired a second pair of missiles directly over his head.

Now he was certain that Carver was mad. He was taking on the Royal Navy.

SIXTEEN

Tomorrow's News

Wai Lin walked slowly down the catwalk as two armed guards followed her. They were almost to the level where they would finish her off and throw her body overboard. Hampered by her ankle chains, she stumbled down the metal stairs of the open work area.

She lay at the bottom of the steps, groaning. The men looked at each other. Was she hurt? One of the men went to help her up, but the other one, more wary, motioned the first man back. He fired a shot next to her head.

"Get up!" he ordered.

Wai Lin struggled to her feet, but the diversion worked. She had managed to get her lockpick earring out of her right earlobe.

It was a clever little device that had been made specially for her by the People's External Security Force's armourer. Both earrings were silver and pictured the yin and yang symbols of opposing yet complementary forces. Quite a bit of Chinese philosophical thought was based on this venerated emblem, and many believed it to possess magical powers. Wai Lin wore them for good luck and, so far, they had worked.

Stamper and several crewmen stood on top of the large machine near the hole that Bond had made with his homemade explosive. Repair material was coming up from the platform below. Stamper looked up at the opening and was astonished to see James Bond's face peering in. Bond was just as startled to see Stamper, who instantly picked up the MP5K that was by his feet. He swung it up, but the hole was empty.

"Seal this up after me. Fast!" he called. He proceeded to crawl through after Bond.

Outside, Bond was ready for him. Stamper pulled himself halfway out of the hole in the top of the hull as 007 took a running jump and landed with both feet planted on Stamper's chest. The German was smashed backward onto one of the sharp, jagged shards created by the explosion.

Bond regained his footing and peered at Stamper. It was too dark to see what damage he had done, and the only sound he could hear was the ocean.

Then, a fresh star shell ignited above, refreshing the dimming light of the one before. Stamper was perfectly still, slumped over with his head down. Bond had started to move on when he heard a low groan come from the German. The guttural sound grew into an ungodly howl that was a mixture of pain and pleasure. Bond watched in amazement as Stamper raised his head and hands, and then pulled himself off the spike. The sadomasochist used the clearly undiminished strength of his arms to lever his body like a gymnast mounting the rings. Such was the agony of his back being ripped away from the metal shard that Stamper laughed aloud. Once free, he jumped up onto the top of the hull without effort. He felt his back, then looked at his blood-covered hand. He licked it appreciatively.

"We are going to have such fun," he said to Bond.

Bond kicked Stamper in the face with a *Mikazuki-geri* maneuver. Stamper absorbed the blow without flinching. He caught Bond's heel and flung it upward, sending 007 crashing painfully to the deck of the speeding ship. Both men were suddenly drenched by the spray from a nearby exploding shell.

"The pleasure will be all yours," Bond managed to say.

The guns on HMS *Bedford* were successful in knocking out the first incoming missile in the air. They were not so lucky, however, with the second wave of fire. One missile got through and hit the ship near the stern. Several crewmen ran to the blaze with extinguishers. Two sailors were taken to the sick bay for smoke inhalation, but there were no casualties.

In the operations room, the alarms screamed and the room rocked.

The captain remained steady. "Slow to five knots."

He got a report from the crewmen, then said to the admiral, "The fire's not bad, sir, but we have to slow down even more while we put it out."

Kelly nodded.

The PWO piped up. "Captain, they're making thirty-two knots. They'll be out of our visual range in two minutes at that speed."

"We'll still have them on radar," Admiral Kelly said,

"even if it's a weak signal. Continue to fire. We've got to slow them down."

Wounded but far from beaten, the *Bedford* resumed her assault on the stealth ship.

The two guards urged Wai Lin toward the railing of the lower work platform. The bottom of the hull was open to the raging ocean between the two pontoons below. One man raised his gun to shoot her in the back.

She got to the railing, then backed away from it toward the guards. One of them put out a hand to push her forward, but she expertly stepped back between them, grabbed their heads, and slammed them together. She then used her own, now-opened handcuffs to lock the dazed men together. Before they could realize what was happening, Wai Lin lifted the guards and flipped them over the railing.

A guard on the catwalk above saw the entire incident. He brought up his gun and opened fire, but Wai Lin scooped up the two guns at her feet and dived away, just ahead of the bullets that ricocheted off the platform behind her.

Wai Lin charged down a lower corridor deep within the ship. Without aiming, she fired a burst of bullets over her shoulder. She rounded a corner, evading the eight guards chasing her. She waited quietly as they ran by, completely missing her. When she was certain they had gone, she emerged and ran the other way. She had to retrace her steps to get to where she wanted to go.

A lone guard turned the corner and met her head-on. Wai Lin used her shoulder to ram the man in the chest. He fell down on his back and she ran right over him, stepping on his face.

• • •

On the stern work platform, crew members succeeded in constructing a two-by-four frame supporting a piece of the black stealth composite material. They raised it against the hole and started to brace it in place.

Carver watched from his office.

"Make sure there are no gaps!" he called into the microphone.

In a moment, the breach was completely sealed. Carver smiled. They were back in business.

The *Bedford* was barely making headway, but she continued to fire 4.5-inch shells by radar. The crew worked frantically to get the fire under control, and the officers studied the monitors intently. The thrill of the hunt had overtaken them.

"Fire's out, sir!" reported one of the crew.

"PWO, back to maximum speed," the captain ordered.

"Sir!" the leading seaman called. "We've lost the target. It's no longer on the radar."

Admiral Kelly looked at the monitor. It was true: the blip was no longer there.

"Damn," he muttered. "It's got to be there somewhere. Keep heading in that direction."

The fight with Stamper raged on. The German threw Bond down on the hull, knocking the breath out of him, but he was still able to roll out of the way of Stamper's foot as it came crashing down.

Although he was fighting with great skill, Bond was receiving the worst of it. The German just wouldn't let up. He didn't seem to tire. At one point Stamper landed seven perfectly aimed blows on Bond's face. Dazed,

233

Bond fell back and almost lost his footing. Instead, he used a handhold to leverage himself, then he leaped up and delivered a beautiful *Savate* kick to Stamper's chin. The brute just grinned and kept coming.

007 hurled himself at his opponent, but the German's foot lashed out and caught Bond in the stomach. He doubled over and Stamper followed up by shoving him with all his strength. Bond went flying over the side of the ship.

Stamper howled at the moon and beat his chest. That felt great! He had done it! He peered over the edge and saw Bond clinging to the side of the boat, six feet below him. Bond's legs were dangling out over the rushing water as the light of the last star shell grew dimmer.

Wai Lin backed into the antiseptic turbine room of the stealth ship, which was dominated by two enormous steam turbines. A large number of metal pipes led into the turbines. The pressure within each pipe was measured by glass-fronted pressure dials.

As she came in, she fired short bursts back toward the doorway. The two turbine crew members fled through the far door as two guards piled into the doorway after her, firing away. Wai Lin was forced to take cover near the turbines, behind the pipes feeding them. She noticed the dials and the valves that controlled them in a row on the turbines. More shots caused her to move. As she retreated past each pipe, she turned a valve. The needles on the pressure gauges began to climb toward the red zone.

She tucked and rolled across the open area between the turbines, provoking bursts of fire that nearly caught her. Once she was concealed again, she started turning the valves on that side, too.

The eight guards continued to advance and cover each other. They didn't notice what she was doing with the valves. As soon as they reached the front of the turbine area, Wai Lin retreated away from them. One of her guns clicked empty, so she tossed it away. She checked the clip in the other—she was down to two bullets.

The guards finally infiltrated the area behind the pipes where Wai Lin had just been. Above their heads, the pressure gauges were now right at the top of the red zone. The pipes were beginning to vibrate with pent-up energy.

Wai Lin fired her last two bullets at two of the pipe valves. They burst, setting off a chain reaction. The other valves also blew, and the room was engulfed in a blast of super-heated steam. It took another minute for the steam to clear, leaving the eight guards cooked as thoroughly as chickens in a pressure cooker.

Wai Lin left the room and emerged onto the lower work platform, then went up the forward stairs of the open area.

Carver and the captain felt the stealth boat slowing.

"We've lost all pressure on both turbines," said the captain, examining the propulsion controls. "We're dead in the water."

"Bad news for us, worse news for China. Get steam back as fast as you can," ordered Carver. He turned to Gupta. "Since we're stopped anyway, we'll fire the missile now."

Gupta didn't want to admit it, but now he was frightened.

Bond was still clinging to the side of the boat, unable to get back to the top. It was easier to hold on now that the ship was stopped, but it was also easier for Stamper to climb down after him.

Twelve feet to Bond's left, the missile launch doors slid open. Bond scrambled to them, with Stamper following a short distance behind.

Bond leaped inside and half-dropped, half-fell from the doors onto the catwalk. He rolled and got up on one knee. Right above him was a small panel, just below the missile doors, with a large green button and a large red one. The panel was marked "Emergency Close/Open." Bond lunged for the red button, but Stamper swung through the doors and smashed him in the sternum with his feet. Bond was knocked off of the catwalk.

He fell into the open area, with the ocean directly below. He managed to grab onto the front of the cruise missile launch tube, which was carefully balanced by supports stretching over the space. His weight on the front made it tilt down slowly, until the missile was pointed straight at the water with Bond dangling from the end of it.

Gupta, in the missile programming area, sat with his bodyguards behind him. He finished punching the keyboard, then looked up at a camera.

"It's ready," he said. "You can fire anytime."

Carver, watching Gupta on the monitor in his office, could also see most of the room his top technical expert was sitting in. He saw the door open and Wai Lin appear behind Gupta.

"Sorry, darling," Carver said into the microphone. "You're too late."

Gupta was confused. "Huh? Darling?" He turned around to see Wai Lin standing there. The three bodyguards went for their guns, but Wai Lin exploded into action. She jumped into midair and delivered a *Tobi-geri* jump kick to one man's face, landed, then swirled her leg around and caught the second man in the chest. She then grabbed the third guard by the head and brought it down hard on her knee. They were out cold.

She turned to Gupta and said, "You ready to handle me now?"

Gupta's jaw dropped open, then he slowly raised his hands in surrender.

Stamper jumped onto the tail of the launch tube. The shift in weight caused the missile to seesaw, so that Stamper's end sank and Bond's lifted. The motion picked up speed, and Stamper was soon swinging from the bottom, over the water. The momentum tilted the missile again—in a few seconds, Stamper's end rose and Bond's end fell. Bond picked the precise moment and jumped off of the missile onto the catwalk below the missile doors. He landed heavily and badly—the fall knocked the wind out of him and nearly broke his arm. It hurt like hell, but he willed himself to get to his feet.

The tail end of the launch tube started to sink fast, but Stamper caught the lower catwalk railing with his ankle, stopping the tilt.

Suddenly, the door to the missile programming room on the forward platform flew open. Wai Lin charged out, propelling Gupta, who was at least three times her mass, toward the railing.

"Okay, okay, I said I give up!" he shouted.

Wai Lin stopped and appeared to consider his plea for mercy. He looked at her with fear in his eyes. Then she shook her head and toppled him over the side. Gupta hit the water like a cannonball.

From his desk, Carver could see on the monitors that Stamper was hanging in the air with his hands on the rear of the cruise missile launcher and his ankles on the lower portside catwalk. He was stretched between these two points and unable to move.

By sheer luck, Stamper's body had lined the missile up with the launch doors. Carver got on the loud speaker.

"Stamper! Stay right there! This will be the best feeling you ever had!"

Carver pressed the firing button. Somewhere embedded in the immense noise of the missile blast, he heard Stamper crying out in an orgasmic wail.

The German henchman was incinerated to a crisp as the missile erupted out of the launch tube. Bond dived for the button to shut the missile doors. He pressed it and simultaneously dived behind a solid steel brace before the exhaust burned him to death as well.

The missile doors shut fast, but the missile was quicker. The entire body of the weapon was out of the doors before they shut, but the edges caught the fins of the missile. They were shorn off as the projectile streaked upward. Without its fins, it started to tumble, and soon exploded into a huge fireball. Pieces of debris rained down around the ship.

Bond ran down the catwalk and met Wai Lin there. The boat rocked as they heard shells exploding alongside. They embraced, but out of the corner of his eye Bond saw a guard.

"Behind you, at two o'clock," he whispered.

Without looking, Wai Lin kicked out behind her and nailed the attacking guard in the face.

"Don't we make a good team?" Bond asked.

Then a shell from the *Bedford* made a direct hit on the stealth ship's bridge. The illumination from the exploding cruise missile had made the *Sea Dolphin II* an easy target.

The People's External Security Force, backed by the Vietnamese police, poured into the CMGN headquarters in Saigon. The guards were helpless against the intimidating soldiers who arrived at the building in two tanks and several jeeps.

The soldiers stormed the building, forcing every employee to gather in a central area while the rooms were searched.

They found General Chang cowering in a women's toilet stall. He was arrested on the spot. General Koh had personally traveled south to take charge of the operation. When he saw Chang being led away by soldiers, Koh reminded him that if he was found guilty of treason, the penalty was a bullet in the back of the head.

Crown Prince Hung and his transsexual underlings didn't hear the commotion. They were too busy dancing to techno-pop in the young monarch's suite. They surrendered peacefully to the guards who burst into the room. The Crown Prince even winked at the officer who handcuffed him, but the gesture went completely unappreciated.

Within ten minutes, both Hung and Chang were on their way to Beijing under armed guard.

The last shell had knocked Carver to the floor of his office. The place was burning. He was disoriented. Something had hit him in the head. He slowly pulled himself up and stood by the monitors. Before he could issue any commands or assess the damage, a single blast of flame burst into the room through the private passage from the bridge. On the video wall, the monitors covering the stealth boat zapped out. Panicking, Carver slammed his fist on the wall, willing the monitors to come back on.

"Damn you!" he shouted. "Work!"

Suddenly, Carver saw his own picture appear on all of the monitors. It was the CMGN broadcast currently being fed to satellites and received by millions of viewers all over the world. Over his face was the title, "Missing?"

He flicked the sound on. Tamara Kelly was saying, ". . . and owner of this network, is reported to have been despondent over the mysterious death of his late wife, only days before the British government's announcement of the eighty-nine-count fraud indictment—"

He snapped the sound off, enraged.

"Damn! They always get the last word!"

Then he saw his own back on other monitors. He turned and saw, through the plate-glass window of his office, Bond and Wai Lin behind the Sea-Vac in its gurney. Its teeth and cameras were pointed right at him.

"The worm turns," Bond said.

He shoved the Sea-Vac through the window. It crashed through, sending shards of glass all over Carver and the room. The obscene contraption snaked slowly toward the Emperor of the Air. It was far worse than a killer whale or the deadliest shark. The rotary teeth whirred with the sound of nails screeching on a blackboard.

The only place they could see Carver was the video wall, where his face grew larger and larger on the monitors, his mouth opening to scream. His cries were drowned out by the Sea-Vac's tremendous noise and the sound of grinding bone. Elliot Carver was sucked into the machine like a carrot into a blender.

Bond and Wai Lin watched the dredging tube bulge with great satisfaction, then they turned and fled. They only had a minute or two before the ship was either sunk or hit again by shells.

Bond caught a running crew member carrying a folded plastic package the size of a suitcase and relieved him of his burden.

"This way," he said to her.

Wai Lin grinned and followed, but not before tripping a frightened guard and stealing an identical package.

Two more shells hit the ship and exploded within, exposing flaming chunks of it.

Bond and Wai Lin made it to the area between the pontoons and dived into the water. They swam under and away from the stealth ship. While they were beneath the surface, they heard a low, resounding boom as the *Bedford* delivered her coup de grâce. They swam with all their might, finally surfacing a safe distance from the crippled ship.

Bond pulled a cord on his package. A CO_2 cartridge hissed and the plastic expanded into a small raft. He spread it out and climbed in.

"May I invite you to—" he said.

Turning behind him, Bond saw that Wai Lin was inflating her own raft.

The *Sea Dolphin II* was listing badly as more shells set off internal explosions. One pontoon was almost underwater. Another shell hit it and the pontoon was pulled under entirely. The ship turned over onto its back and, with a last massive, sighing explosion, finally sank.

Everything was quiet except for the sound of the waves and the bubbling foam that marked the spot where the sea shadow had gone down.

The two secret agents from opposite sides of the world reclined, each on an individual raft, but they held the sides of their rafts together so that their heads were in intimate alignment.

"You sure you don't want to join me?" Bond asked.

"It's just, sometimes a girl wants to wake up in her own raft," she said.

"I understand. You want to paddle your own canoe."

"Well, I suppose we could paddle together."

"Tonight we'll paddle in your raft, tomorrow we'll paddle in mine."

A ship's siren sounded nearby, but Bond and Wai Lin paid no attention. The *Bedford* was probing the floating wreckage and oil slick with a searchlight. It would take a while before the little rafts were found.

A voice on a loudspeaker called out, "Commander Bond! Are you there, sir? If you can hear us, make a sound or show a light. Miss Lin! Can you hear us? This is the Royal Navy . . ."

The searchlight beam swept past the lovers without hitting them as they brought their mouths together.

"Mmm, I've decided that banking is definitely the life for me," Bond said as he climbed into her raft and she pulled him down on top of her.

She laughed and said, "You know, I thought this day would never end. Now I'm not so sure I want it to."

He kissed her again and said, "That's all right. Forget about today. Tomorrow belongs to us."

Wai Lin wrapped her legs around his waist and unzipped the front of his wet suit. Then she sighed and said, "That's the best news I've heard in a long time."